HIT for FREEDOM

THE HIT SERIES
BOOK TWO

MARGARET MCHEYZER

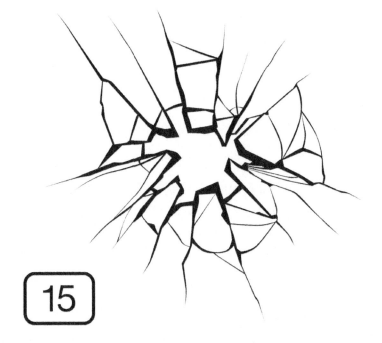

15

Email: hit_149@yahoo.com

info@margaretmcheyzer.com

HIT FOR FREEDOM

I may be a woman but I'm lethal.

Secrets.

Games.

Danger.

Ben Pearson is the cop I was contracted to kill, but I couldn't do it. Something happened between us and instead of doing what I was paid to do, I hunted the people who paid me to kill him.

I couldn't stay and continue to put Ben's life in danger, so I disappeared. Well... *I was supposed to.*

On the way out of Bankstown Creek, I crossed paths with Katsuo Vang. He's powerful, controlling and evil to his very core. He's also interested in me, and something or someone in my hometown.

Now I'm playing a dangerous game to get close to Katsuo and figure out what he wants in my hometown.

However, he doesn't trust easily. But I have patience and I'm willing to lay low until it's time to show him I'm a ruthless adversary.

The problem is, there's a lot of information I don't have and I hate going in blind. But that's what I have to do in order to protect Ben and Bankstown Creek.

The further I fall down this venomous rabbit warren, the more deadly secrets are hidden.

The worst from the one man I never thought would betray me. The person I saved all those months ago.

The one who makes my heart beat faster. Ben...

Stay calm and slay...that's what Anna would do.

PROLOGUE

BEN PEARSON

I should have known she wasn't going to be at the house. Something in my gut told me she wouldn't be there.

I sit in the cruiser outside the station, frustrated and angry that after all these months, she's disappeared again.

I'm angry at myself for not disclosing my other life to Anna before she vanished. The very least she deserved—*deserves*—is my honesty. If she had been at the house, I would have had the opportunity to finally tell her. To let her into all the parts of my life. But she's stubborn and demands control of everything, no other possibilities. It's always her way or no way.

Since she's been gone, I've reached out to so many people my family knows in order to find her. But the thing about Anna is that it doesn't matter how hard anyone searches for her. They won't find her if she doesn't want to be found. I chuckle and shake my head as I stare at my phone. "You don't find Anna, Anna finds you," I whisper to myself.

My phone ringing startles me out of my heavy headspace. I look at the number, hoping it'll be unknown—meaning Anna again. My shoulders sink when I see it's my sister. "Emily," I say as I lean my head back against the seat. "How can I help my favorite sister?"

"You better not tell Claire I'm the favorite, she'll kick your ass."

Emily makes me smile. "Yeah, she would."

"Listen, you need to come home because there are a few things happening."

I sit straighter and flick a look over toward the station. "Is everything okay?"

"It is for now, but I need you and Claire here." I take in a deep breath. "Before you go freaking out, everything is fine," she reiterates.

"I can fly in Friday night."

"Claire's flying in on Thursday, so that works."

I hesitate for a moment. "Are you sure everything is okay?"

"Oh my God! Listen to you. You're always worried about everything."

My brows fly up as I tilt my head to the side. "Do you blame me?"

"You can relax a bit, Ben. We've got it covered. Honestly, you're going to give yourself high blood pressure. We're in this together, all three of us."

I take a deep breath and calm my frantic mind. "I know, but I worry about you and Claire."

"So, other than you stressing over business, how are you?" she asks in a softer voice.

I look down at my knee and flick invisible lint from it. "I'm fine," I reply with a lie.

"Have you forgotten about what's-her-name?"

Although I told them about Anna, I didn't tell them everything. "Obviously. Anna is a figment of my imagination. She never existed."

"See, this is good. You need to get yourself laid."

"Just like I don't ask about your sex life, I'm not going to talk about mine either."

She clicks her tongue, and I can imagine she's rolling her eyes already. "Whatever."

"I have to go, but I'll see you on Friday night." I hang up and take a breath before leaving the cruiser to head back into the office.

Grace smiles up at me when she sees me. "Boss," she says and adds a nod when I walk in.

"I'll be in my office." I walk past her and down the corridor and to the right into my office. My desk is organized chaos, with papers stacked all across it. I take both my phones out of my pocket and place them in the top drawer as I sit and look at the work load.

I have to forget about Anna and move on with my life. Even with all my connections, I haven't been able to find her.

I want to move on, but I damn it, I can't. I need to find her.

And soon.

CHAPTER ONE

ANNA

"Is my house ready?" I ask Agent as I drive toward Bankstown Creek.

"It's ready. I'll send you the address." My phone pings indicating Agent has texted the address for my new cabin in Bankstown Creek. "It was no small feat either."

"What did you find on Katsuo Vang?"

"Same as yesterday, nothing. That name doesn't exist, not here in America nor anywhere around the world. No Social Security number, no bank accounts, no address. He doesn't even have a driver's license."

"Which means he's hiding something."

"I'll keep working on it, and I'll see if I can find anything. I'm owed some favors, so I'll call them in and see what I can get." I can hear Agent's disappointment in himself.

"Good, do so. I need to know who I'm up against." I hang up and increase my speed as I drive toward Bankstown Creek.

If no information can be found on Katsuo Vang, that means I'm going into this completely blind. I don't like working without having all the information, but I also know that there are times when I need to be prepared for the unpredictable. And this is one of those times.

The drive to Bankstown Creek is long and tedious, giving me ample time to think about Ben and Katsuo. I don't want to cross paths with Ben, but it's inevitable at some point.

I pull up the address Agent sent me and punch it into my car's navigation system once I reach the outskirts of Bankstown Creek. The drive to my new cabin takes me an additional twenty minutes, and I'm happy to see the cabin is nowhere near where the skeleton of the old cabin remains.

Thankfully, this cabin is off the beaten track and well hidden, which means Ben won't be able to find it. I turn my car off and get out, making sure to stretch after the long drive back. I open the trunk of the car, take out my bag, and head up to the front door. Agent calls me as I approach the entrance. I scan my thumbprint to gain entrance. "Second door to the right is your weapons room."

I wheel my suitcase in and leave it by the front door. "Is the layout the same as my other properties?"

"Similar. Only major difference with this one is the kitchen also has a concealed weapons drawer."

"It does?" I ask as I walk over to the kitchen.

"Take a step to the left and turn to face the fridge." I do what Agent asks. "Under the lip of the counter." I feel around under the counter beside the fridge. "There's a fingerprint pad, can you feel it?" My finger skims over a small cold square. "It's your pointer finger." I press my index finger over the pad, then a section at the back of the counter slides up. Inside are two semi-automatic handguns.

"Two guns?" I ask as I roll my eyes.

"They're there for an emergency."

"Next time you add something like that into the design, add a drawer with several weapons."

"Your weapons room is fully stocked as you like it," Agent says, hurt in his tone. "The windows are bulletproof glass too."

I hang up, take my earpiece out, and lay it on the counter. I walk into my bedroom and look around. It's virtually a carbon copy of my other homes, the ones we've built from the ground up. I sit on the edge of the bed and open the new laptop waiting for me. I hack into the Bankstown Creek Police Department personnel files and search for Ben's roster. I need to be careful when I'm here to ensure we don't cross paths too early.

Not because I don't want to, but because I can't. Being the person I am, I can't allow myself to put Ben's life at risk. He's a civilian and an innocent; if I drag him into my world, then there's no turning back.

He wouldn't survive in my world.

My shoulders droop forward as I stare at the roster with Ben's name on it. I can't do it to him. I'm here for a job, and that's to figure out who Katsuo is and what he's doing in Bankstown Creek.

I pull my shoulders back and close my laptop. I reach over to the bedside table and open the top drawer where I find several burner phones. Standing, I return to the kitchen and find the business card Katsuo gave me with just his name and number. I dial it and lean against the counter as I wait for him to answer. "Yes."

I roll my eyes as I straighten. A chill passes over my body as I fake a smile. "Hi, Katsuo?" I say in a small, innocent voice.

"Anna Moore, I've been thinking about you."

My stomach tenses and I feel dirty just having to be on the phone with him. But I have a job to do, and I can't do it efficiently if I know nothing about him or why he's here. "Have you?" I add a small giggle. "I like that I've been on your mind."

"Tomorrow night," he starts.

"What about it?"

"Dinner," he says matter-of-factly.

"Are you asking me out on a date, or are you telling me you'll be eating dinner?" I can play the damsel, although it's not something that comes easily to me.

Katsuo laughs, then huffs into the phone. "What's your address, and I'll send a car for you."

Hell to the no. "Ha, nice try, Mister," I lighten my tone to play it off as someone who's overly cautious. "But I don't know anything about you, so no, you won't send a car for me. On the other hand, I'm happy to meet you somewhere."

He chuckles again. "You can never trust a stranger," he says cryptically. "Although, after our date tomorrow night, I'm hoping you'll no longer consider me a stranger."

Gag me. "Wh-where should I meet you?" Being vulnerable takes a lot of work for me.

"There's an airstrip off the highway as you pass the gas station where we met. Do you know it?"

It's not a public airstrip, which worries me, because why would he know about it? "Yes, I do."

"Good. Meet at the hangar at five. And, Anna, I don't like to be kept waiting. I'm not a patient man." He's attempting to set the rules for any future relationship he believes we might embark on.

"Of course. Five and I won't be late."

"Good."

"But before I forget..." I add.

"What is it?" his tone elevates, as if he's irritated.

"I don't like to be kept waiting either."

Katsuo clears his throat. "You're going to be a handful, aren't you?" He doesn't give me a chance to reply before he adds, "Until tomorrow, Anna," and hangs up.

He makes my skin crawl. Yes, until tomorrow. When I'm going to have to refrain from hurting him to find out as much information as I can.

Ben

"Ben, the new assistant chief is here," Grace announces after she knocks once on the door.

I look up and see her smirking. "Why are you smiling?" I stand from my desk and walk around to meet Grace.

She leans into me and whispers, "She's cute." Then she waggles her brows.

"I'm sure she is. But, no, don't try and set me up with anyone." We walk down the corridor toward the front.

"But..." I silence Grace with a stern look. "I just thought..."

"Don't," I warn.

Her shoulders droop forward as she releases a small sigh. "I won't," she glumly agrees not to attempt her matchmaking skills with me.

Standing by the front counter where Grace usually sits, stands a woman whose hard stare demands I tear my eyes off of her. "You must be Adele," I say as I extend my hand.

"Yes, sir." She steps forward and takes my hand in hers.

I wasn't expecting anyone as beautiful as Adele. Her department photo doesn't do her justice at all. "If you'd like to follow me back to my office, I'll brief you." I drop her warm hand and step backward to indicate she should follow. "We're a small department here in Bankstown Creek."

"Yes, sir, I'm aware."

Once in my office, I gesture for Adele to sit in my guest chair and close the door before walking around the desk to sit down. "You graduated at the top of your class from the academy. Well done."

Adele's forehead crinkles and she folds her arms in front of her chest. "I graduated a few years ago and have been in the field since. My record should speak for itself," she says with sass.

Her arrogance reminds me of Anna. I must admit, I like it, but I refuse to allow her to top me like this. I cock a brow and sit back in my seat. "Around here we follow a chain of command, and by that, I mean we speak to each other with respect. If you think coming in here and throwing your weight around will make any of my team respect you, then you can go back to where you came from. I don't want you here." I run my tongue over my teeth, waiting for her response.

Adele keeps eye contact with me, until she doesn't. Her cheeks turn pink and she lowers her chin. "I'm sorry. I'm used to playing defense all the time."

I find that hard to believe, but I'll give her the benefit of the doubt. "Apology accepted. How are you settling into Bankstown Creek? It can take some getting used to, especially considering you came from a big town."

"More like a city," she says and adds a small laugh. "You're right, it's a lot slower-paced than I'm used to, but it's also a welcome change." Adele lowers her eyes and releases a soft sigh.

Something about Adele tells me she needs this. Maybe she's gone through something traumatic and she needs a break. Or it could be something more sinister. I'll do a thorough background check on her and make sure she's not another Ethan Martelli.

"The station is small but we all mesh together well. If there's a problem with any of the officers, you need to let me know. You and I share a cruiser, because we only have four for the station."

"Okay," she says as she nods her head. "Is there a desk for me anywhere?"

I stand, as does Adele. "You certainly do have a desk. I'll show you." We head out of the office to the pool of desks, and I gesture to the one in the back corner. "This one is yours."

"Ben." Marsha tips her head as she sits at the desk she shares with one of the night shift officers.

"Marsha, this is Adele, our new assistant chief."

Marsha stands and holds her hand out to Adele. "Hi." She smiles at Adele, who returns it in kind.

"Hey."

"I have some work for you to do, so I'll bring out the files I need you to go through." I head back into my office, grab one of the piles, and return to place them on Adele's desk. Miles is already hovering and speaking with her. "Miles," I say as I stand beside him.

He instantly straightens and takes a step backward. "Hey, Ben." He clears his throat and attempts to smile, though it's stilted and awkward. "I was about to head out and do some..." He points toward the front door. "Um..."

It's easy to be affected by Adele because in truth, she's quite stunning. I get a feeling she doesn't put up with nonsense, either. I respect that, and the boys had better respect it too or we're going to have a problem on our hands. "Good," I say as I stare at a flustered Miles.

He lowers his chin and backs away from us. Adele looks around and walks over to grab one of the files from the stack on her desk. "Can you not do that?" she asks in a low voice.

"Do what?"

She peers over her shoulder again and says, "I can handle myself."

I give her a slight nod. "My apologies." Maybe I overstepped my mark, or maybe I didn't. Either way, she doesn't want me interfering. Adele comes across as cold and emotionless, not cocky or abrasive. I leave Adele to work while I head back to my office. I open the drawer and take out my personal phone.

Dialing the number, I wait for Claire to answer. "Boss," she says.

"You know I hate it when you call me that."

She snickers. "What do you want? I'm closing a deal."

"Can you run a check for me?" I wait a few seconds for her reply. "I take that as a yes. I'll send you the information I have on her."

"Her? Oomph, who is she? Tell me all about her," Claire teases.

"It's not like that."

"Is she hot?"

"Claire," I say sternly.

"Ugh, you're such a party pooper." I roll my eyes. "Anyway, yeah, send me whatever info you have on her."

"I want to make sure she's not another Ethan Martelli. I can't stress to you how important it is we don't draw any more attention to us."

"Oh, she's a cop. You could've just said that."

"She's taken over Ethan's position."

"Ahh, see, now you're making sense. I'll find whatever I can on her."

I know Claire is no Agent, especially considering Ethan slipped through my guard for so long before Anna discovered who he was. "We need to keep a tight rein on who's working for me here."

"Yeah, yeah, I know. Anyway, I'll see you Friday." I hang up and place my phone back into the drawer. I open the laptop and search Adele's name in the police database in case I missed anything the previous times.

It doesn't look like I have, and now I need to wait for Claire to find what she can, in case the past is attempting to repeat itself.

I dare say though, if I was dealing with another Ethan Martelli, Anna would show up. Is it bad that now I'm kinda hoping Adele isn't who she claims to be just so Anna returns?

CHAPTER TWO

ANNA

I look through my wardrobe and find the tightest, sluttiest dress I can. Katsuo isn't going to respond to a conservative me, but in a tight dress, with a good pair of heels and attention to my lips, he'll be putty in my hands.

And right now, I need to find out who he is. He'll be more relaxed if I make him believe I'm more body than brains. I hate having to stereotype women like this, but one thing I've always known is that sex sells. It sells a promise of what could be rather than what is. The fact I have a killer figure and I'm attractive means I can be even more lethal.

As I flick through the hanging dresses, my eye is instantly drawn to a long, red strapless dress with a slit that goes all the way to the top of my thigh. I lift the hanger out and place it on the bed. "Yep, you'll do." I find a pair of black heels to complement the dress and a black clutch to finish the outfit. The only problem is I won't be able to sneak any weapons with me, because this dress will betray any bumps or lumps. The outline of a gun would be a giveaway, so against my better judgement I'll have to go unarmed.

I grab a quick shower before I start getting ready for this *date* with Katsuo. "Date," I snicker to myself as I style my hair into soft curls that cascade over my shoulders. "More like a mission." This is part of the job, being able to masquerade to gain an advantage.

Once I'm ready, I check myself out in the mirror. The red dress does wonders for my figure, and I love how it clings and accentuates all my curves. I grab my clutch and car keys and head out.

Driving to the hangar, I'm careful to make sure I'm not being followed, though other than Katsuo, no one knows I'm here. The one thing I hate is not being armed, because I have no idea who Katsuo is or what he's capable of. Time will tell though.

I pull up outside the hangar and there's a man with a fully automatic gun standing at the entrance. He sees my car, lifts his finger to his ear, and nods once. He walks over to me and taps my window.

This is where I need to be the softer, more vulnerable version of myself. *Time to play.*

"Oh," I say in a soft voice and bring my hand up to my neck while glancing at his obvious weapon. "Um, I think I may have made a mistake."

"Don't be alarmed, Miss Moore."

"Oh, um." I visibly swallow and flutter my eyelashes at him.

"This is only for your and Mr. Vang's protection."

I clear my throat and nod slightly. "I'm just really nervous around guns."

"Mr. Vang is running behind, if you could please pull your car into the hangar someone there will direct you."

I hesitate before offering him a small smile. "Sure. Thank you." I wind my window up and slowly drive through the gates. There's a jet sitting on the runway with a red carpet rolled out. So, where is he taking me? Hmm. I carefully look at the number of people milling about, armed and waiting for Katsuo's arrival. Why hasn't Agent been able to find anything on him? There has to be a reason.

A different man is standing rigid by the hangar. He has the same type of weapon the other guy had. He lifts his hand and stops me from driving any further. He rounds the car and tries the handle, but the car doors are locked. "Unlock the car please, Miss Moore," he instructs with a roll of the eyes and a small huff. I unlock the doors and he opens it for me. "Please step out of the car," he says in a bored, almost mechanical voice. He holds his hand out for me to take.

"Okay," I whisper, putting on the pretense that I'm overwhelmed and terrified. I snatch my clutch off the seat and reach for his hand to take. The instant I do, the hair on my arms stand to attention while that all too familiar turmoil in my gut makes it churn. At some point, I'll have to take this guy out. All in good time.

"Ma'am, please make your way to the jet." He points to the aircraft waiting for me. I do a double take and furrow my brows. "Mr. Vang is running late. Please." He gestures with a sweep of his hand toward the jet again. "Your keys, please."

"But my car..." I look between him and my vehicle.

"It's in safe hands," he says and chuckles condescendingly. "If anything happens to it, Mr. Vang will replace it." He cocks a brow. "With something..." he clears his throat. "Better."

I hate how this guy is talking to me. But, in all fairness, I'm deliberately not showing him my hand. God no, he's on the bottom of the food chain. I need to find out who Katsuo is, first and foremost. "Thank you." I offer him a shy smile and take a moment to glance at my car, then him, silently begging him to be gentle.

I couldn't care less about the car, but I need to be consistent in my naivety. "I'll look after it." I'm sure he will. He's probably been instructed to fit it with a tracking device, which is going to make it difficult for me to remove without them knowing. It will be tricky, but not impossible.

I turn and start walking toward the jet. A woman who I assume is the hostess appears and walks down the stairs. She meets me at the end of the red carpet with a bright and genuine smile. "Welcome, Miss Moore. Mr. Vang is en route and should be here within the next few moments. Would you like to follow me aboard?"

"Oh, thank you." I carefully make my way up the stairs while keeping a cautious eye on everything happening around me.

"Welcome aboard, Miss Moore. My name is Lindy and I'll be looking after your and Mr. Vang's needs. Would you like a champagne to start?"

I sit in the opulent leather seat and look around the aircraft. The thick black carpet is spotlessly clean, while the gold trim sparkles with no sign of it being tainted by fingerprints. "Thank you." I offer her the same kindness in return.

She hurries away and returns within moments holding a silver tray with a single flute of champagne. "Mr. Vang is arriving on the tarmac. Is there anything else I can get for you?" she asks with a warm smile.

"No, thank you."

She gives me a small smile and returns the silver tray to the galley before heading down the stairs to greet Katsuo. My skin tingles as my stomach contracts and eases. Damn, I can't believe how nervous I am. Not because I'm afraid, but because I don't have access to my weapons. If I'm put in a position where I have to kill, I will. But it would be easier if I had even one of my guns.

Lindy appears and a man walks in behind her. He has massive, broad shoulders and he's wearing a shoulder holster holding two guns. My body instantly relaxes when I see them. He might be a big guy, but his weapons are easily accessible, which means I'll be able to get to a weapon if I need it.

Katsuo walks in behind the security guy who breezes past me as if I don't exist and positions himself at the rear of the plane. Katsuo sees me and smiles. I place the untouched champagne on the small shelf under the window and stand to greet Katsuo. "Wow," he says when I stand. "Wow," he repeats as he drags his eyes down over my body.

"Wow yourself," I say as I look him up and down.

"You look absolutely amazing." Katsuo signals for me to sit again and positions himself beside me. He turns in his seat and allows his eyes to shamelessly hover over my breasts. His tongue peeks out as he runs it over his bottom lip. I have no idea who he is, but I wish I could kill him and get it over and done with. He's looking at me like I'm prey, and I hate it to my very core. "I'm a lucky man."

I smirk and roll my eyes. "It's just a date, Katsuo. Who knows, I might not like you after this." I giggle and lightly touch his arm.

"Or I might kidnap you and keep you chained to my bed." *Ugh, who says shit like that?* I remove my hand and bring it up to my mouth while smiling. He leans over and places a kiss to my cheek. "You think I'm joking?" he whispers in a deep husky voice.

I think I'm going to throw up. I lower my hand to my lap and look over to him. Tilting my chin down, I look at him from beneath my lashes. "Where are you taking me for dinner?" I ask, completely avoiding his gross statement. I'll fucking kill him if he tries any of that shit with me, and I'll deal with the consequences later.

Katsuo lifts his hands and skims it down my cheek. *God, is he made of cheese?* "There's a cute little restaurant I go to often."

"And where is this cute little restaurant?"

"Ottawa." He sits back and lifts his hand to summon Lindy. "Scotch."

"Certainly, Mr. Vang."

He checks her ass out in the tight skirt she's wearing and catches me staring at him. "As I was saying, it's in Ottawa."

"We're going to Canada?"

"We are." He nestles back in the seat and looks forward, waiting for his beverage. "Are you worried?"

"A little."

The corner of his lip tugs up in a small smile. Ah, I see, he relishes instilling fear into people. I'm quickly picking up on the angle I need to work if I'm going to find out what business he has in Bankstown Creek, and if it involves Ben.

"Mr. Vang," Lindy chirps as she hands him his scotch. As she walks down toward the front, his eyes are again firmly set on her ass while he lifts the glass to his mouth. I wish I could slam the palm of my hand into the bottom of the glass to smash it into his mouth. I'd hold his head firmly in my hands and make him swallow the shards of glass, knowing they'd perforate his esophagus on the way down. It takes every ounce of strength to hold back and not live out the fantasy.

"This is your captain speaking. Please prepare for takeoff," a woman's voice says over the plane's sound system.

"Wow, Ottawa," I say, trying to distract myself from all the delicious things I want to do to Katsuo.

"Have you ever been?"

Well, there was this one time I was paid to take out a cartel's rival. "Only briefly once, many years ago."

"What did you do when you went *many years ago*?"

I killed someone, motherfucker. "I'm a headhunter, so it was for work. I liked what I saw though, and I was hoping one day I'd return."

The plane does a short taxi before taking off. "A headhunter? Whose head do you headhunt?" He chuckles as if my work means nothing.

"People I'm paid to track down," I cryptically say and smirk.

"And do you always find the person you're looking for?"

"I always find the right person for the job."

"So…" he pauses and looks over his shoulder to the guy who entered the plane first. Katsuo snaps his fingers and holds his hand out. The guy stands and hands him an envelope. He holds the envelope and angles his body to look at me. "Do you know what this is?"

"No, but I'm sure you're going to tell me."

"This, my dear Anna, is your background check." I have to remind myself not to kill him yet. "You see, in my line of work, I have to be extremely careful with who I let into my life and become involved with."

Don't kill him. Don't kill him. "I'm not sure I know what to say or how to react. That's an invasion of my privacy." I glance at the envelope he's holding. "I didn't do anything like that on you. Maybe I should," I challenge.

Katsuo throws his head back and releases a big belly laugh. *Hold it together, Anna, you're doing this for Ben.* "I doubt someone like you would even know where to start." Condescending asshole.

"What's that supposed to mean?" I cower back into my seat, almost like I'm sulking.

"It means you're too sweet and innocent to know about my world."

Thank God. This is the first hint as to who he is. I'm not entirely sure I'll be able to withstand an extended period of time with him. "Your world?" I ask with deliberate innocence.

He ignores my question and opens the envelope. I try to look over at it, but he shields it from me so I can't see. "If you have nothing to hide, then you needn't worry about what's in here." His eyes scan over the paperwork. I'm not worried about what's in there, because it'll be what I want him to know. It's what Agent has put in place over the years to ensure my public profile is innocent. "I see," he says and clicks his tongue against the roof of his mouth.

"What do you see?" I lift my hand and nibble on my fingernails.

Katsuo continues to read the paperwork, completely ignoring my staged nervous plea. He's playing a power game. He wants to become the power player in our dynamic as early as possible, so that I learn to obey him. It's all about intimidation and control. "Hmmm."

"You could ask me anything, and I'd tell you. But continue looking at the stupid background check," I huff and turn my back on him.

"Don't you dare turn your back on me," he barks with authority. *Yep, I'm getting under his skin.* I feel the side of my lip turn up in a smirk, but I keep staring out the window for dramatic effect. He grabs my shoulder and spins me to look at him. "I said, don't turn your back on me."

"What do you expect me to do? Sit here and watch you read about my life? Great date, Katsuo." I roll my eyes and sigh louder, making sure to really push his controlling nature. "I should've said no to this ridiculous date. Pffft, if that's what you even call this. You've barely said anything to me."

"You wouldn't have turned me down, because I'm a man who gets what he wants."

Excuse me, but I think you're showing your misogyny. "You have no right to speak to me like this." My challenge is to push him and evoke every possible reaction I can. I need to see what he's capable of, but, I also know I'll have to accept responsibility for all his reactions.

His jaw tightens as he stares at me, attempting to silence me with a demonic glare. "You're damn lucky I don't..." he pauses and takes a breath.

"Lucky you what?" I push as I defiantly cross my arms in front of my chest. "Huh? Lucky what?"

He lowers the papers to his lap and clenches his hand into a fist. Any second now, he's going to hit me, and when he does, I can't react by pummeling his head in and killing him. If I do that, I'm no closer to the reason he's taken an interest in Bankstown Creek or who he is. He unwinds his hands and abruptly stands. Katsuo leaves and walks toward the back of the plane. I hear a door slam, then something smashing.

I know I'm being watched so I cower down in my seat and bury my face in my hands.

"Miss Moore, can I get you another drink?" I hear Lindy's soft voice.

I lift my head and blink several times as I take in a deep breath. "Just some water please?" I ask in a small voice, but loud enough for her to hear over the roar of the engines.

She offers me a small smile and a nod before walking to the front. Lindy quickly returns with a bottle of water and a glass on a silver tray. She cracks open the water, and pours it into the glass. "Here you go." She hands me the beverage. "Is there anything else I can get for you?" She flicks her eyes to the back, then to me. She's trying to warn me, without actually saying anything.

"I'm okay, thank you. It's just a misunderstanding," I say in a small voice, hoping she'll relay how I'm taking responsibility for his misogynistic outburst.

Lindy nods once and heads down the aisle toward the front. It takes Katsuo another half an hour before he returns and sits beside me. I don't say anything; I simply glance over in his direction before turning to look out the window. The tension is real, but only because I'd love to put a bullet between his eyes right now. However, I know I need to hold back on doing so.

"Please don't speak like that to me again, Anna. I don't handle disrespect well, and I can't be responsible for my actions if you mouth off again."

"I'm sorry," I say as I keep looking out the window.

"Excuse me?"

Asshole, he wants me to face him and apologize. I turn and keep my eyes downcast submissively. "I'm sorry for making you angry. But, if you want someone who'll bat her eyes and accept being ignored, then perhaps this won't work out." I gesture between us. "I just don't like being ignored."

He lifts his hand and places it on my arm to gently rub up and down. "I'm sorry too, Treasure." *Treasure?* Ugh, incoming cheese alert. "I shouldn't have spoken to you the way I did, nor should I have left. But, please don't push me. I have a bad temper, and I'm not a man who takes those things well."

Oh boy, what a dick. If it wasn't for Ben, I would've killed him already. "Let's just get to Ottawa, and we can enjoy ourselves." I smile and gently place my hand over his.

Katsuo's eyes lower to my lips, then back up to my eyes. Shit, he's going to go in for a kiss, and as much as the thought of his mouth on mine makes my stomach churn, I know it's inevitable. "That shade of red will look good around my cock."

"I have the lipstick in my bag if you want to use it to draw on your cock," I say with a straight face.

Katsuo stares at me, completely stoic before bursting into laughter. "That mouth of yours will get you in trouble, Anna Moore." He lifts his hand and grabs my jaw, keeping me in place before leaning over and kissing me. The kiss is wrong, and makes me want to scrub my mouth with sandpaper to get the feel of him off of me. But this is also part of being a honeytrap. I need information to keep Ben and Bankstown Creek safe, and if this is what I have to do, I'll do it.

I deepen the kiss and push my body closer to his. It quickly escalates with Katsuo's hands pushing the split of my dress to the side and instantly attempting to get into my panties. "Hey," I say as I scoot backward in my seat. "I'm not that type of girl, Katsuo."

He wraps his arm around my waist and slides me closer to him. "You can't make me hard then say no." Katsuo grabs my hand and places it on his cock. "See, I'm hard."

I snatch my hand back and turn to face forward. "I'm not that type of girl," I repeat.

Out of the corner of my eye, I see him visibly gulp and shake his head. "I'll accept that, *for now.*"

He makes my skin crawl. *Don't kill him, yet, Anna. Don't kill him,* yet. Thankfully, the three remaining hours of the flight go by without another incident. I've yet to find out who he is, or what he does, though.

We land at an airstrip where a black limousine is waiting for us on the tarmac. With his hand to the small of my back, Katsuo guides me toward the car. "This really is a sexy dress you're wearing tonight."

Duh, I know. "Thank you." I look over my shoulder toward him and smile.

As I slide into the car, I notice a dark SUV beyond the gates and down the road. To me, the dark SUV stands out. Perhaps it belongs to Katsuo and his men, however the twisting of my stomach tells me it's more sinister.

"You're going to love where I'm taking you," Katsuo says. "The restaurant has the best steak I've ever eaten."

The dark SUV is mostly concealed behind the thick brush. This is what keeps me at the top of my game. I see things others would miss. "It's such a pretty night, isn't it?" I angle myself to look up at the dark sky and to sneak a look behind us.

"I'm a little surprised." Katsuo's grip on my thigh startles me.

I turn toward him and tilt my head to the side. "About what?"

"You seem relatively unaffected by all of this." He makes a sweeping gesture with his hand to indicate his affluence. "You're not interested in money?"

I have enough money to last me several lifetimes. "You must've seen how much I have in the bank."

He chuckles. "Yes, you have a modest amount," he says with a patronizing grin.

"I think half a million dollars is quite healthy." There's also all the other money I have stashed away.

He dismissively shrugs. "It's adequate, I guess."

"I'm self-sufficient and don't need or want anyone else's money."

"You also haven't flinched at my security detail. Which..." He clicks his tongue to the roof of his mouth. "...worries me."

"You're worried that I'm not reactive enough? If a person has a private jet, then that person has money, and when money is involved, protection is required. So, no, I'm not intimidated by wealth." I flick a look at his security sitting in the front. "Nor men with guns."

Katsuo cocks a brow and lets out an audible "hmm." He reaches for my hand and entwines our fingers. I hear the engine roar, then feel the impact as our vehicle is smashed into from behind.

I turn to see the SUV smash into us again, letting out a small scream for added effect. The limousine hurtles forward as the SUV pulls back, then increases its speed to ram us a third time. Neither the limousine nor the SUV will be able to withstand another slam like the two we've already endured. Katsuo has his phone in his hand yelling and screaming.

The SUV smashes into us once more, causing the limousine to drift off the road. I look at the driver and see he's slumped over the wheel. I reach for my guns and instantly hate myself for leaving them behind.

Fuck.

Katsuo reaches inside his jacket and produces a pissy little gun, unlike my weapons, which are locked away in the weapons room at home. *Double fuck.* If that's all we've got to protect us, we're dead.

"Do you have another gun?"

"Only this one." Great. "Backup is coming."

Sure enough I hear the deep rumble of vehicles approaching at lightning speed. We're quickly surrounded by three dark SUVs similar in make and model to the one that rammed us. Katsuo takes in a relieved breath and wrestles with the door to open it. These are his SUVs. So who the hell smashed into us?

I slide out behind him and watch as men from the other SUVs all jump out with weapons strapped to them. There's a lot of yelling and instructions given in Japanese. I pick a few words up, but I'm not skilled in the language.

Everybody is on high alert as they fan out in a protective formation around us. Although I'm calm, I have to stay in the character of someone who's new to this world. I wrap my arms around my torso and hunch my shoulders over. I try to muster tears, but tears don't come naturally to me. My tears stopped the day Dad was killed.

One of the guards flicks his gaze toward me and Katsuo instantly turns. He tucks his itsy-bitsy little toy gun into the back of his pants and walks toward me. He wraps me in his arms and kisses my temple. "Treasure, you're trembling."

I'm not, but whatever. "I'm scared." I keep my voice small and frail.

"I'm sorry you had to see that. Are you hurt?" I slowly shake my head. "I saw them but I thought they'd attack at the restaurant." He pulls me closer to his body. "Take care of it," he instructs his men as he flicks his eyes to the crumpled mess of the car.

The driver of the SUV that rammed us has been pulled out of the car and is pretty banged up. There's a gash in his head where blood is oozing. Katsuo's men push him to the ground and yell at him several times. I hate not understanding a language. *Note to self: learn several languages, including Japanese.*

They lay boots into his side and the man groans from pain. One of them drags him up by his shirt and forces him into a kneeling position. I know what's about to happen. This is a roadside execution.

"Do you know who that is?" *Please give me something.*

"Come." He nestles me closer into his body and walks us toward one of the SUVs. He opens the back door and waits for me to slide in before he and one of the heavily armed guards enter.

"Who is he? What does he want?" I'm trying to add some panic into my voice so I don't sound so damn calm. *Come on, Anna.*

The driver who rammed into us takes off and darts around Katsuo's small army of security. I turn to see them put a bullet in the back of his head. "Don't." Katsuo lifts his hand and places it on my chin to turn my head.

I have to react appropriately. I blink several times and think of the moment my father was killed. When I saw him tied to the chair, Nox standing over him with a gun to his head. The pure fear in Dad's eyes. I lower my chin and stare at Katsuo's chest as that horrible memory that's been burned in my head replays over and over. My stomach churns with the pain of having failed my father when he needed me most.

I can't let that happen again with Ben. I need to muster my strength and fucking cry. I bury my head into my hands and drag myself back to those moments of how I felt. The paralyzing fear of being helpless while my father was being held as leverage for me. *I couldn't save you. I'm so sorry.*

I lower my hands and wipe at my eyes. "I feel sick, Katsuo. I think I need to go home."

"Just, come to dinner and I'll explain everything."

"I'm not sure I can eat." I suck in a breath and wipe at the last of the few tears that have managed to fall.

"Ah, good." He looks out the back window and inhales deeply. "We're safe, I promise."

I follow his line of sight to see the other cars have now caught up to us. "I'm scared."

"Of course, you would be. But, I promise, we're safe now, no one can get to either of us."

"Me? Why would someone want me?"

"You're with me now, Anna," he says matter-of-factly.

"What do you mean by that?"

"I'm a man who has a lot of influence with certain *things*."

Ugh, can you stop being so cryptic? I shake my head and lift my shoulders slowly. "I have no idea what you're talking about."

"Anna." He runs his tongue over his teeth and looks at me. "I'm Gokudo."

Right. Well, this is fucked. "Oh," I say as I turn to look out the window. Gokudo is commonly known as the Yakuza. I've been contracted by the Yakuza in the past for tricky hits.

I'm going to have to be careful or this is going to end up messier than it has to be.

Chapter Three

Ben

Things have been stirring in Bankstown Creek for a couple of weeks. There's a sense of dread, an eerie heaviness, hanging over everyone, and none of my CIs have any information, or they're too fearful of what's coming to tell me.

Emily and Claire have always had their ear to the ground and are able to stay on top of most things, but now the three of us are in the dark. Something is happening, but what, none of us know. It's moments like this I wish our parents were still alive. Because of their years in the game, they had a longer reach. I stare at my computer screen as I think about a range of things. Anna being prevalent and filling most of my mind.

I shake my head to dislodge thoughts of Anna and look away from the screen. My phone ringing snaps me out of the murkiness in my mind. I open the drawer and reach for my cell to see Claire's calling. "Miss me, little sis?" I say as I sit back in my chair and look up at the ceiling, pushing Anna as far away as I can.

"People are scared," she says.

"I know." I close my eyes and rub at the mounting tension across my brows.

"No one is talking. And, there's been a downturn in demand."

I open my eyes and sit forward. "What do you mean?"

"There has been a significant decline."

I clear my throat as I sit straighter and stare once again at my computer. "Have you spoken with Leon James?"

She groans and huffs at the same time. "Ben, I've tried," she says in a small voice. "He's a piece of shit, and he's not talking." I furrow my brows as I try and figure out a plan moving forward. "We need to find out what's happening. If shit keeps moving forward like this, someone may be moving in and before we know it, we'll be out." Claire says, and judging by her tone, she's angry. So am I. I understand why, especially when it comes to our family business.

"My shift finishes in a few hours. I'll FaceTime with you and Emily so we can try and figure this crap out."

"Whatever is happening is fucked," Claire pointedly snaps.

"I know," I reply with equal venom. "I know."

"It's not good for business."

I scrub my hand through my hair and nod. "Claire, I said, I know."

"If we're seen as weak and losing our touch…"

I cut her off, already irritated by her constant, on-edge shrill. "I know," I say once again. "I have to go."

"Ben—"

"I have to go." I disconnect the call and haphazardly toss my phone back in the drawer and lean back in my chair. There's a constant whirl of uncertainty and worry pumping through my mind.

"Let me go, you fucking bitch!" I hear someone yelling from out in the front of the station. I push out of my chair and go to investigate who's yelling and why. I walk out to see Adele dragging a middle-aged drunk man behind her. "You're a bitch," he spits toward Adele as she continues to drag him toward the cells.

"You alright?" I ask as I watch her handle him with ease.

"He can sleep it off."

"She punched me," the guy groans. "Look." He tilts his head toward me, showing me a bruise quickly blooming around his eye.

"Come on, Ted, you can sleep it off in the cell," Adele says in a deadpan voice as she continues to manhandle him.

"I'm pressing charges," he slurs. He turns his head and looks at me. "Ben, Ben. Tell her, she's a bitch."

"You know him?" Adele asks over her shoulder.

I follow her as she tugs Ted toward the cells. "Kind of." I half shrug.

"Come on, Ben. Come on," Ted drunkenly rambles as he pleads with his eyes for us to let him go.

"Right, Ted, you can sleep it off in here." Adele opens one of the cells and pushes him in. "Back up to the bars so I can take the cuffs off," she instructs.

On shaky legs, Ted struggles to turn but after a good few minutes of him trying to stop swaying, he backs up and she takes the cuffs off of him. We both walk out and leave Ted to sleep. "What happened?" I ask, indicating toward the cells with a slight jerk.

"I came out of the supermarket and there was Ted, trying to get in his truck to drive home. He dropped his keys, and I went over to him. When I took the keys, he started cussing and even swung at me."

"He swung at you?"

Adele flicks her hand dismissively. "Twice."

"Twice?"

"I hit him when he came at me for a third time. Put him on his ass," she says stoically. "I handcuffed him, and helped him up and put him in the back of the cruiser. He just needs to sleep it off. He'll be sore tomorrow."

"I'll call his wife," I say as I head back toward my office.

"I thought you said you don't know him." Adele follows and leans against the doorjamb of my office.

"I don't, but this is a small town and I'm the police chief, which means I know *of* nearly everyone. Ted's had to sleep in our cells once or twice before. His wife kicked him out of the house once because he'd forgotten her birthday. Doris is a spitfire, but they're both harmless."

"Does he drink a lot?"

"Once a year, on the anniversary of their kid's death. He gets totally drunk at home." My forehead crinkles as I type out a text on the computer for Grace to get me Ted and Doris's number. "I think it might be that time of the year."

"How sad," Adele whispers. "Imagine losing a child." She shakes her head and lowers her chin. "How sad," she repeats.

A message appears from Grace with the number. I pick up the phone and dial it. "Hello?" her voice trembles as if she's been crying.

"Doris, it's Chief Ben Pearson."

"Is Ted okay?"

"He's been brought in drunk."

"He wasn't driving, was he?"

"He tried to, and he took a swing at one of my officers. He's sleeping it off in a cell."

"I'm so sorry," she says in a small voice. "Today's been a hard day."

I was right; today *is* the anniversary. "Look, I'm not going to press charges, but you can't come get him until tomorrow. His truck is..." I look up to Adele. "At the grocery store," I say, waiting for Adele to nod her confirmation. "Have you got an extra set of keys?"

"Yeah, I do." Doris sniffles and with a quivering voice she whispers, "Thank you. I'll come by in the morning to get him."

"Look after yourself, Doris."

"I will."

I hang up the receiver and look to Adele. "You're not pressing any charges against him?"

"He's having a hard time, and they barely ever give us any trouble. Sometimes we need to give people a break. Especially on days like today."

Adele pushes off the door and clicks her tongue to the roof of her mouth. "Small towns, huh?"

"We're a different breed of people down here, Adele."

She smirks and walks out of my office. While she's walking away she says, "Don't I know it."

Thankfully, my day is nearing its end, but I still have a pile of paperwork I need to finish before I can head home.

I've been home for a couple of hours doing some research. I barely have time to pour myself a scotch when my phone vibrates with Claire's face. I hit accept and leave the phone on the kitchen counter. "You're late," she scolds me.

"I was busy at work," I say as I pour myself another scotch and walk back to sit at the barstool.

"I'll get Emily on the call." The screen splits into three windows, the last third is black until Emily's face appears. "Hey," Claire says.

"Um, I can't get word from anyone about what's happening. One of the runners was mouthing off, and, well." Emily shrugs and looks off to the corner.

"What's that supposed to mean?" I ask.

"He was a problem, now he's not," she casually replies.

"Emily." I point at her but then close my eyes and rub at the tightness near my temples. "Don't go stirring shit until we know what's happening."

"I'm not letting some little pissant speak to me like that," Emily shoots back. "Our family built this, and I'm not letting anyone take it away from us. We just need to figure out who's undercutting us, so we can annihilate them."

"We're not going to do that if you go taking matters into your own hands."

"He's right, Em," Claire agrees with me.

"I'm done sitting on my hands doing nothing. We need to move on this fast, before we're destroyed and there's nothing left."

"You need to calm down before you give yourself a fucking heart attack," Claire says. "Just chill."

Emily snaps a deadly look at the phone. "Did you just say for me to chill? How can you sit there so fucking calmly?" Her face is reddening as her eyes grow larger and bulge with anger.

"Calm the fuck down," I snap, irritated by both of them. "We need to figure out what's happening before we attempt to clean up whatever mess this is."

"The one thing I know for sure is that we need to keep our anonymity. We can't act out of frustration and kill people because we don't like what they're saying." Claire pointedly looks at Emily. "There are only a handful of organizations that can create this kind of pandemonium so quickly.

We need to work our way through them and figure out who's coming to destroy us."

"I've reached out to the Irish and they're adamant they have no idea who's doing this," Emily says. "I believe them too."

"They're good customers, so they have no reason to lie to us," I add. My other cell vibrates in my pocket. I hold my finger up to my mouth and place the phone down on the counter. "Yeah," I answer.

"Sir, we need you to come in," Miles says with a short, shaky voice.

"Everything okay?"

"I think it's best if you come and see for yourself. I'll text you the address."

I look at the time on the microwave and silently groan. It's nearing midnight, and I've already had a scotch. "I'll be there soon," I say before hanging up. I pick up the phone and look at both my sisters. "I've gotta go back to work."

"I've got a meeting with the Germans," Claire starts.

"I've got a meeting with the Italians," Emily adds.

"Okay, for now, don't either of you do anything that could compromise us." I purposely look at Emily. "Stay in touch," I say.

My sisters all disconnect and I head to my room to change.

As I'm locking my house, my phone rings again and I hit accept without looking at the number. "I said I'm coming," I snap.

"Not without me."

I instantly recognize that beautiful, sweet voice. "Anna," I say with a big grin.

"We need to meet," she says.

"Where are you?"

"Not tomorrow but the next day, you're not working. We need to meet then." She completely avoids my question. I'm not even surprised.

"What's your number? I'll call you." At least this way, I'll have her number. *For now.*

She chuckles into the phone. "I'll get in touch with you." Damn it, she's fucking avoiding the question.

"Anna..."

"I have to go," she whispers in a tight voice.

Is she in trouble? I need to find out so I can protect her. I shake my head as I get in my car. Protect her? She doesn't need protecting. But God damn it, I want to be the one who keeps her safe. She doesn't need to be so strong all the time. I smack my hand on the wheel and relax my tense jaw. "Fuck!" I briefly close my eyes to regain my composure. I haven't heard from her in what feels like forever, and her phone call was a small tease. An infuriating torment.

It takes me a few moments to clear my head, and when I do, I put the address into the navigation system and drive the twenty minutes to one of the smaller neighboring towns we also cover.

The street itself is like any normal suburban street you'd find anywhere in America. Maybe even around the world. The street is wide and lined with aged trees that have low hanging branches.

The police cruisers with flashing lights ahead direct me to where I'm supposed to be. I park and exit the car. "Boss," one of the officers greets as he lifts the police tape for me to duck under.

I walk up to the house and find Adele walking out. "You're here too?"

I glance at the front where the door is supposed to be and crinkle my forehead. I cross my arms in front of my chest and jut my chin toward the house. "What happened?"

She opens her notebook and starts reading what she knows. "Jason and Michelle McClennan are dead. They own this house, and the hardware store in Chester Park. Married eight years, and by looks of things they kept to themselves. She's twenty-nine and he's thirty. Neither have any type of record, not even a speeding ticket. We've talked to a few neighbors and they all paint the same picture. A quiet, hardworking couple."

"The door's been blown straight off."

"Yep. And, they were in bed when it all happened."

I tilt my head to the side as I scratch at my jaw. I walk in expecting to find at least Jason dead near the front. "They were in bed when this happened?" I look around the living room, and back to the door jamb. "Where's the door?"

"Forensics has already tagged and bagged it."

"Where's the bedroom?"

"Upstairs, toward the back." Adele points.

I take the stairs two at a time hoping I can get to it before the bodies are moved. Forensics is in the room tagging everything. The bodies are lifeless on the bed. The wife is lying on her stomach with part of her skull missing from a bullet to the back of the head. The husband is on his back, with a smaller head wound, dead center between his eyes. Another bullet is in his chest.

What are we missing?

The door was blown off the hinges which would've made a loud enough commotion to wake them. "Who called it in?"

"One of the neighbors heard something and peeked out of their window to see the door blown across the front lawn. They thought it may have been a gas explosion so they called nine-one-one."

"Has anyone interviewed the neighbor?" I ask.

"Marsha spoke to the neighbor, and he's given her nothing. He didn't see anything, nor was he looking. Like I said, he thought it was a gas explosion."

I look around the room and tap my finger to my chin. "Get back to the station and run a check on their financials."

"You think they were in trouble somehow?" Adele asks.

"Doesn't it strike you as peculiar that a neighbor heard the explosion, but these two were in bed and didn't hear a thing?"

"Yep, I've been thinking the same thing too. I can't smell gas, so it can't be that. How do two people sleep so heavily that they don't hear an explosion?"

"Exactly. Besides, we know this was a hit." Shit, was this Anna? Did she do this? I look down at the bodies and blink several times.

"What is it?" Adele asks as she reads my concern.

"Nothing." I quickly push that thought to the side. "I um..." I look at the bed where the two are dead and run my hand through my hair. "I'm going to stay behind and try to piece this together."

Adele's brows furrow before she gives me a small nod. "I'll head back to the station and run financials. I'll look at the mortgage, and see if there's anything that might not look right." She hovers for a moment before I turn to stare at her. I don't say anything. Instead, I give her a questioning look. "Okay then." Adele gulps, looks around once more, then leaves.

This is going to be a long night.

CHAPTER FOUR

— • —

BEN

I'm damned exhausted. I didn't return home until after six in the morning. I ended up with two hours' sleep and now I'm back at the station.

I'm making myself a coffee when I hear Adele approach from behind. "Morning," she says in a sleepy, croaky voice.

"Yeah." I glance over my shoulder at her. "Coffee?"

"Sure." She leans against the wall and lets out a massive yawn. "Did you sleep?"

"A couple of hours. You?"

"Same." Adele blinks several times and yawns again. "Sorry."

"No need to apologize. Did you find out anything in the financials?"

"I should have a report for you in about an hour. But..." She exhales a long sigh as she shakes her head. "I don't get it, at least not from the preliminary information I found." I hand her a coffee, then lift mine and start walking back to my office. "I'll have the full report to you soon."

"Thanks." I continue heading toward my office and close the door before I sit and fire up my computer. I look at the stack of paperwork I have to do and lift my coffee, sipping on it. I'm not in the mood to be here, nor am I in the mood to do this paperwork.

Before I even realize, there's a knock on my door. "Yeah?" The door creaks open to reveal Adele. "What's up?"

"I sent you an email with what I found attached."

I look at the screen and open the internal department mail. I click on the file Adele has sent. She walks in further and sits opposite me as I read what she's written. "Nothing at all in their financials?"

"Nothing I could find," she corrects.

I flick my gaze up to her, then back at the screen. "The hardware store looks profitable, nothing over the top." I scan the money on hand, and what they have in the bank. "They have a modest mortgage, their health insurance is all paid up to date, nothing owed there." I shake my head.

"I can't help but think that this case seems all wrong. Everything about it is bizarre."

I look up at Adele and nod my agreement. "No past records at all?"

"Not a single thing. The only thing I found in all of this is they tried for a baby but neither were capable, so they put in an application for adoption."

I blow out a loud breath and shake my head again. "How sad. They won't be getting that call now, will they?"

"This is..."

"What about family?" I ask as I keep scrolling through her report.

"Both are only children, and both have deceased parents." *Wow.* "I know right? How sad. They literally only had each other."

"They're too clean to be killed for no reason at all. I was at the house until early this morning and nothing was disturbed, nothing seemed to be taken. We're missing something." God, I really hope this has nothing to do with Anna. "Unless..." I look up at Adele and chew on the inside of my lip. "A serial killer?" I shake my head as I think about it.

"I searched for any deaths in this state that resembles what we have with the McClennans, but I didn't find anything at all." Adele pushes up off the chair and takes several steps backward.

"Something isn't right. The door was blown off the hinges and neither the wife nor the husband came down to see what the commotion was. That's what's stumping me," I say.

"I'll keep digging to see if I can find something, but on the initial investigation I can't see anything that might even resemble a red flag."

"Thanks. Close the door on the way out." Adele leaves and closes the door behind her. I look at her report again and try to piece this puzzle together. This is a fucking mess, and I need to figure it out for many reasons.

Mostly because I don't want a serial killer running around Bankstown Creek.

Nor do I want anyone looking into my business.

CHAPTER FIVE

ANNA

"My beautiful Treasure," Katsuo says when I answer the phone. I shake my head. I can't wait until I can gouge his eyes out. He hasn't let me into his inner circle yet, but I'm working on it and suspect I'll be in it soon.

"Morning," I say in a chirpy voice with a sour taste of disgust coating my tongue.

"What are your plans for today?" I tactfully look out the window of my house and see the car he assigned to me parked down the street. This has been tricky, trying to navigate with Katsuo constantly wanting to know everything about me. The fact that men "discreetly" follow me around everywhere has proven to be challenging for Agent and me. Thankfully, Katsuo hasn't quite crossed the line where he's bugging my phone or keeping me with him every moment of every day.

"Well, as you know I've taken some time off work, and I thought I might go do some shopping." Cliché, I know, but I can lose his men and it'll make them look incompetent, not like I've given them the slip.

He clears his throat. "Where will you be going?"

"I'm not sure, why? Do you want to join me?" I tease with forced heavy smokiness to my voice.

"I um…" He clears his throat again. "I'm not even in America, but if I was, then I'd love for you to model things for me."

Ugh, can he make my eyes roll any harder than they already are? I've already seen the inside of my skull several times in this short conversation. "Oh, where are you?" I ask attempting to pull as much information from him as I can.

"I'll have one of my men come with you, and whatever you want they'll pay for it."

"I'm not your kept woman, Katsuo. I can afford to pay for my own things."

"There's my little spitfire." His carefree, yet condescending laugh shoots straight to my nerves making my blood boil with irritation. "My men will be with you."

"No need. I'm a big girl who can look after herself."

"It's cute you think you can protect yourself. Treasure, I'm the big bad wolf and what I say goes."

He's seriously the most nauseating man I've ever dealt with. Okay, maybe not the *most*, but close enough. I can't wait to kill him. My hand tightens around the phone, but I manage to close my eyes and take several deep yet silent breaths. *Just breathe, Anna. His time will come.* "I'll make you a deal," I say, adding an innocent giggle.

"And what's that?"

"One man, and he has to stay outside the store. I don't want him following me around and creeping out the other shoppers. It's unfair to the other women. I don't want them feeling insecure."

Katsuo chuckles and I can imagine he'd love the feeling of being in full control over me. If only he knew I'm setting him up to tear him down. I just need him to trust me enough to let me into his inner circle. "I'll accept your terms on one condition."

My stomach churns with whatever ridiculousness he's about to spit. "You need to buy a classy, sexy dress, because I have a meeting and you'll be coming with me."

I fist pump the air with happiness. *Finally.* "Well, that'll cost you extra."

"Money's not even a consideration. Your bodyguard has a card with no limit. Spend whatever you want on anything you want. But a tight, sexy dress is a must. I want all the other men to look at you like they want to rip the dress off your tight body, and to look at me like they want to kill me because you're on my arm."

What a dick. "Awww, aren't you cute?" I mime sticking my finger down my throat. "If slutty is what you want, then slutty is what you're going to get." If this is my in, I'm going to make sure I'll be a welcome distraction for him and the men in his meeting. "When's the meeting?"

"Why?" It's clear by his instant coldness that he's defensive and suspicious.

"Because I need time to prep," I say, clearing up his wariness.

"Oh, well, I'm back tomorrow and the meeting is the night after. Be ready for ten."

"I'll be ready."

"Although, I'd prefer to see you before then."

My skin crawls. "Maybe you will, maybe you won't," I tease enough to drag a desperate groan from him.

"You're a naughty girl, aren't you, Treasure?"

Balk. "You'll need to wait and see. Anyway, I have to get ready so I can go in search of this dress you want me to buy."

"My man will be there soon."

He must think I'm a complete idiot not to see the car outside my newly acquired house in the small town neighboring Bankstown Creek. Agent worked wonders to find this place, buy it, and have it furnished so that when Katsuo decided I was his, my house would seem normal, and like I've lived here for a while. By "normal" I mean without a weapons room that anyone can stumble upon. "He can wait outside until I'm ready to leave," I say with sass.

"I wouldn't expect anything else from you. He'll be driving you wherever you want to go."

I hate being treated like a porcelain doll. But this is what Katsuo wants, and it's what I have to be for him until I tear my mask off and show him who he's dealing with. But for now, I'll be dainty, soft Anna. Not "I'll tear your eyes out of your head and crush them beneath my bare feet" Anna. I hang up, look at the car once more, then call Agent.

"How's my favorite assassin doing?"

"If I could end my suffering by killing him right now, I would," I say as I begin to strip so I can take a quick shower. "Do you know what he wants me to wear to his meeting?"

"You're in! You're going to a meeting?"

"Yep, and the prick wants me to wear something classy yet slutty."

"Isn't that a contradiction in itself?"

"Classy yet slutty." I groan as I unbutton my jeans and push them down over my hips and thighs. "But, yes, I'm in. Well, I hope he's not fucking with me." I turn the speaker on and toss the phone on the bed as I strip down. "Have you found anything on what he's doing in Bankstown Creek?"

"No, this guy is playing his cards close to his chest."

I take the phone and walk into the bathroom. "And here I thought you were good at your job."

"Ouch, that one hurt." I can imagine Agent clutching at his chest with imaginary pain. "Remember that job you did about three years ago?"

I know exactly which one he's talking about. "Yeah."

"The one where—"

"I know which hit you're talking about, Agent. What are you getting at?"

"I could reach out to the client and ask some questions—"

"No," I cut him off as I shake my head.

"But—"

"No," I repeat. "We keep this low-key. You're not to tip anyone off about this, because once I take him out, I don't want the weight of the Yakuza on me."

"But—" he attempts to argue, to get his point across.

"I said no."

A few seconds of tension passes between us. "Okay, I'll keep digging."

I hang up and leave my phone on the cabinet before turning the shower faucets on.

"Mr. Vang has expressed his intention for me to stay close to you," the big, beefy bodyguard says.

"And I told him I don't want you in the stores I go to," I reply. His stoic, cold glare tells me he's not going to leave because I've asked. I run my tongue over my teeth as I cock a brow and stare at him outside the boutique I'm going to enter. I chose this mall because I know it's going to be busy soon, which means I'll be able to slip past him and go to Ben. "No?"

"No, Miss Moore."

I slide my phone out of the overpriced bag I use to appear normal and dial Katsuo. "My Treasure."

God, I hate the stupid nickname he has for me. My name is Anna or, as I prefer, 15. "I told you I don't want him in the store with me. He's riding my ass like an oozing hemorrhoid. Get rid of him."

"An oozing hemorrhoid?" Katsuo questions slowly.

"Yes, like it's burst and it's smeared everywhere. I'm two seconds off telling you to get rid of him for good. He stays outside, or…"

"Or what?" he threatens in a low voice.

Or I'll fucking slit your throat, *motherfucker*. "Please," I say, toning down my irritation.

He intakes a sharp breath, then exhales a drawn out groan. "He stays by the door in case he's needed."

"Thank you. Now, stop bothering me, I have a sexy dress to buy." I smile, knowing the bodyguard is intently watching me.

No quicker do I hang up than the bodyguard receives a call. He lowers his head. "Yes, sir," he says. I wait until he's off the phone and slides it back into his suit jacket pocket. "I'll be waiting outside, ma'am. If you need anything, just yell out and I'll be right there." He positions himself to the right of the door, with his back up against the wall.

"Thank you." I walk into the store and dawdle long enough to know I'm not going to find anything that fits the description here. I need to build the trust of the bodyguard to relax for a moment so I can slip out the back of a store, just not this one.

The next hour is spent with me going into several stores and charging whatever I buy to Katsuo's credit card. This is all a ploy to get to him. For Katsuo to trust me enough to think I'm willing to comply with his wishes yet have a little pushback from me.

"Here you go." I give his bodyguard the bag with the hooker heels I bought. They make my legs look great but damn, they're uncomfortable. Give me a pair of steel-toed boots any day of the week. Although, the point of a stiletto can take out an eye and pierce deep enough to sever the jugular at one-point-five inches below the skin.

"I'm not here to carry your bags," he says as he looks at the bag I've already forced into his hands.

"I'll just call Katsuo." I open my purse as I see him flinch and straighten. I continue to take my phone out of my bag and begin to dial Katsuo's number. I bring the phone up to my ear.

"What now?" he asks, adding a carefree chuckle.

"Your bodyguard doesn't want to hold the bags." I stare at the big, beefy guy and half smile.

"He's not there to carry your bags."

"Then I don't want him." I want to be a thorn in Katsuo's side, because he needs to know I'm not a pushover. A man like Katsuo likes the challenge, knowing I have a smart and sassy mouth.

"You drive a hard bargain."

I smile widely in front of the guard. "Thank you." I slide my phone back into my bag and hear the bodyguard grumble as he answers his phone.

I don't bother hanging around to hear the one-sided conversation; instead, I head toward the next store. When I walk into the boutique, I quickly find a dress that is exactly what Katsuo has asked me to buy. The bodyguard stands at the door to wait for me. I hand him the bag and head over to purchase the intimate apparel the dress requires. Katsuo has made it no secret that he likes seeing me in cute underwear. This is all a means to an end. I hate having to have sex with him, but I know there's no chance I'd get this far if I didn't. And finally, it's all paying off and I'm going to a meeting. Maybe now I'm going to know what his business is and what I'll need to do in order to keep both Bankstown Creek and Ben safe.

But tonight, I need to sneak out of the house so I can see Ben, because there's no way I'll be able to get past the guard now.

"There's a car waiting for you on Station Street," Agent instructs as I jump the back fence.

Thankfully, I'm moving under the cloak of darkness. Katsuo's men are positioned in front of my house, about three houses down. "What am I looking for?" I ask, staying hidden as I pass through the neighbors' yards.

"It's a white Toyota Corolla."

"Which side of Station Street is it on?" I carefully glance down the street, making sure I stay out of sight. I duck down behind a car parked in a driveway and wait for Agent's instructions.

"On the right."

While still squatting, I look toward my right and can only just make out a car parked down the road. "Could you park it any further away?"

"I could've had it delivered to your house," he replies with obvious snark.

Smart-ass. I look around once again to check that I'm in the clear before I sneak toward the car. Keeping low, I'm as invisible as possible. I don't want to alert Katsuo's men. With my heart in my throat, I make my way over to the car. "Keys?"

"It's unlocked, and the key is under the driver's side floor mat."

I look around once more, then try the handle, confirming it's unlocked. I slide into the car and lift the mat to find a single key. The moment the ignition fires to life, I'm already taking off out of here, though still keeping a close eye on my surroundings. "Keep an eye on the house, and let me know if anything happens."

"Of course, 15."

I hang up and take off toward Ben's.

I let out a long sigh of relief when I make it to Ben's without being followed. I pull into his driveway and sit staring straight ahead for a moment as I take several long breaths. I lay my head on the wheel to calm my rapid heartbeat. "Pull yourself together," I scold myself. Lifting my head, I look at Ben's front door and pull my shoulders back. There's not one available moment to feel vulnerable. Because if I do, I may as well surrender right now. And I'm not a woman who lays her guns down without a damned fight.

I open the car door and cast a cautious glance down the street before I head up to the house. I try the handle and find it locked. I look around again, knock lightly, and lean up against the wall to wait.

The door opens and the moment Ben sees me, his eyes light up as a warm and welcoming smile erupts. "Anna." He sweeps me into his arms, against his taut body, and kisses me with desperation. "I've missed you," he whispers against my lips. He kicks the front door closed with his leg and moves us into his family room. I relax against Ben's tall, sturdy frame as he holds me while kissing me. Ben pulls back and cups my face in his warm hands. "I was worried you wouldn't come."

I smile as I step back and glance toward the floor. One of the things I love about Ben is how he wears his heart on his sleeve. It's sweet and refreshingly different. "I had to see you," I say.

Ben gestures toward the sofa, but I shake my head and wet my lips. "Why did you disappear?" he asks with a controlled voice. "I looked for you." Absentmindedly, I let out a small chuckle. "I know," he says. "You don't find Anna, Anna finds you."

I step backward until I'm leaning against the armchair. I lower myself to sit on the arm. I swallow several times, attempting to lubricate my dry throat. Why am I so nervous? "I left because..." I purse my lips and roll them together. "It's too dangerous for you if we're..."

"Together?" he interrupts my slow sentences. "I can handle myself."

"You were shot, and I thought you were going to die."

"Look." Ben walks toward me, but I lift my hand to stop him from approaching. Ben's step instantly ceases. "There are a few things we need to talk about."

"I know. It's why I'm here." I swallow once again and look up to Ben as his brows draw tightly together. I shake my head and bring my hand up to wave it once. "Let's get to that later," I pause and take a deep breath. "What's happening at work?"

"Work? Really? I haven't seen you for months, and you show up now without any explanation as to where you've been to ask me about work? You left without any warning."

I run my tongue over my teeth as I stay seated on the arm of the armchair. "I did that to protect you."

"I don't need protection."

"I'm an assassin. You're a cop," I say bluntly. "We could never work as a couple."

"Because you're stubborn, and you think you know what's best for me without even asking!" I snap my cold gaze up to stare at him. My blood ices through my veins as I fist my hands into balls. "Don't stare at me like you want to kill me, because we both know, I'm right. You *are* stubborn."

I stand to my feet and take several steps toward the door. "This was a mistake." I shouldn't have come here. I should've kept to the shadows because that's where I do my best work.

Ben's on his feet and lunging toward me. He wraps his hand around my upper arm and pulls me back to him. I can easily overpower him, knock him on his ass and put him down. I know he doesn't want me to go. "The only mistake was that you left me." Ben lowers his head and smashes his mouth into mine. He weaves his fingers through my hair and fists a handful of it to keep me close to him. "You're not going anywhere." He pushes his hard body into mine, making me step back until I find the wall behind me. Ben releases my hair and roughly drags his right hand down my body, squeezing my breast, then continues down to grip my thigh and tease it up over his hip. "You've been gone far too long," he mumbles against my mouth.

In a moment of vulnerability, I find myself whispering, "I've missed you so much."

Ben stops kissing me and leans his forehead on mine. "Don't leave."

"Ben..."

"No." He kisses my forehead. "If I have you for only a moment, then I'm not going to argue with you." Ben steps back and in one fluid movement, he leans down and swoops my body over his shoulder.

"Hey!" I protest.

He smacks my butt as he takes me toward his room. "Nope," his tone has turned easy with a hint of silvery husk. "I refuse to go another moment without my cock being buried deep inside you."

"If you insist," I tease. He smacks my butt again as he enters his bedroom and tosses me on the bed like a ragdoll. "As much as I like seeing you in a suit, I do prefer you naked." I lean on my elbows and gesture toward his shirt. "Take it off." The mood has lifted to something easy and fun.

Ben slowly unbuttons his shirt and I watch as he puts on a little striptease for me. "Like this?" He flings his shirt open and stands like a superhero looking to the side with his chin up, chest out, and his hands on his hips. I burst into laughter at his pretentious stance. "Are you laughing at me?"

I confirm with a resounding, "Yep."

Ben's brows slowly rise as he tilts his head to the side. "Well, maybe I *won't* fuck you."

I hesitantly lift my shoulders. "It's not like I can't take care of myself." I make quick work of shimmying out of my black pants and opening my legs so Ben can watch. "I can do this without you." I sit up on the bed and snake my hand down to my panties, where I push them to the side and rub my fingers over my clit. "See, I can do this without you."

Ben steps forward and falls to his knees in front of me. "Let me." He tries to swipe my hand away, but I waggle my finger at him. "Please," he begs as he moves his face closer and closer to me.

I lift my leg off the bed, place my foot to his chest, and push him back. "You can watch."

"Fuck," he grumbles as he sits back on his heels and watches while I pleasure myself. "Jesus," he says as I finger my clit. "Let me at least have a taste."

"You can watch," I say again as I watch him watching me. He licks his lips and sits closer.

"A little taste." I plunge two fingers into me, making Ben growl with want. "Fuck this." He leaps forward, grabs my wrist, and pushes it to the side. Without hesitation, he buries his face in my pussy, licking and slurping like a starved man who's been handed a feast. "God, you taste like I've died and gone to fucking heaven." He grabs my hips and drags me closer to his mouth.

Ben is relentless as he licks and tongue fucks me until I'm on the edge of coming. "I'm gonna come."

"Come on my face, baby. I want your cum all over me." He attacks my pussy with renewed passion. "One taste isn't enough when it comes to you."

I grind my hips against his face, using his mouth and tongue for my own pleasure. Judging by his groans it's clear he's enjoying that himself. God only knows, so am I. "I'm coming." I grab his hair and hold his head in place. I love rocking my pussy against his face.

"That's it. Give me every drop of your cum," Ben mumbles.

My body shudders as my hips keep vibrating against his mouth. "Jesus," I groan as my body becomes hyperaware, then begins its descent into pleasure. "That's it, keep doing that."

Just as my heart stabilizes, Ben sits back on his heels and smirks at me. He wipes his mouth with the back of his hand and licks me off his finger. "Fucking delicious."

"Fucking hot," I say as I watch him suck on his finger. "Come here." I gesture for him to stand, and he does. "Strip."

"Yes, ma'am. But I want to see your tits." He looks at my top that's still on. I rip it off and unclip my bra, throwing it over the side of the bed. "Beautiful." Ben climbs onto the bed and instantly takes my nipple into his mouth. He flicks it several times with his tongue as he settles between my legs. I reach down to grab onto his cock and guide it toward me. "Oh

God," he groans as he impales me. "I've missed you." He thrusts into me, and in this moment, I'm not 15. I'm not an assassin. I'm not on a mission. I'm just Anna with Ben. Our bodies are perfectly entwined as we seamlessly move together. "I'm not going to last." With only a few more strokes, Ben comes undone. He collapses on top of me and kisses my neck. "That's what not having sex for months does. It makes me lose my load in minutes."

A laugh tears through me as Ben rolls over and lies on his back. "I shouldn't laugh, but..."

"I'll do better on the next round."

Standing, I head toward his bathroom. "You can eat pussy pretty well, it's not really necessary for you to do anything else."

"It's all about you, is it?" he calls once I close the door.

I open it and stick my head out. "Duh," I say, then close the door again.

"Smart-ass," he yells. Once finished in the bathroom, I waltz out and lie on my stomach next to Ben. He turns on his side and draws lazy circles on my back. I can feel the change in the air, the heavy questions are coming. "Don't go."

I blink several times and let out a small sigh. "I'm working on something, so I can't stay."

His brows furrow as he breaks eye contact with me. Here it comes. "I need to ask you something."

"What is it?"

"There were two hits a couple of nights ago. A husband and a wife..." his voice trails off. He doesn't want to ask, but he's going to. I see his Adam's apple bob. "Did you have anything to do with it?"

"Are you going to arrest me?"

His eyes snap up to mine. "So you did have something to do with it?"

"You're being a cop again, Ben. If you answer my question, I'll answer yours."

"No, I wouldn't arrest you. But, I do want to know if it was you."

"It wasn't. But, tell me about it. Maybe I'll recognize the MO of someone I know."

"Married couple, late twenties to early thirties who were shot in bed. Nothing was disturbed or taken, the house was clean but the front door was completely blown off of the hinges."

"The front door was blown off?" How bizarre. Ben nods his agreement. "And they were shot in bed?"

"Like they were asleep."

"And it wasn't staged?"

"Nope."

"And nothing was taken?"

"Not a single thing."

"What did they do for work?"

"They owned and operated a hardware store."

"You've looked into their financials?" He nods again. "How clean are they?"

"Squeaky. Nauseatingly clean. Not even a parking ticket. They literally were the picture perfect, wholesome American couple with the white picket fence and all the bells and whistles."

"Kids?"

"Nope, no kids."

"So the kids didn't get themselves in trouble and Ma and Pa took the brunt end of it. It was a warning then."

"A warning? To whom? From whom?"

"I suspect it was by their boss. I can guarantee they're not so squeaky clean, I think you'll find their hands are quite dirty. Whoever killed them could've cleaned the scene and simply vanished. But that's not what this is about. They were killed, and the door was blown off the hinges so that the neighbors would call the police to find the bodies."

"The door was blown off after they were killed?"

"Why draw attention to a crime unless they want the crime to be discovered?" Ben sits up in bed as he runs his hand through his already disheveled hair. "What?"

"To have your mind. Adele and I thought they blew the door off then entered."

Why do I feel instantly angry when he mentions a woman's name? "Who's Adele?" I mimic his posture and push up to sit on the bed. "Who is she?"

"My second. She's new." I cock a brow. "Are you jealous?"

"You say her name easily. Is there something going on?"

He shakes his head in denial. "What? No."

"I have no right to ask, I'm..."

"You don't have to be sorry."

I jerk my chin up and stare at him. "I'm not sorry," I quickly add.

"Then you're jealous."

"No!" I vehemently deny.

The left side of his lips tugs up and he scoots over to sling his arm over my shoulders and pull me into his body. "Nothing is happening between Adele and me. Besides..." He snickers. "...I value my life too much and I'm way too scared of you."

I look up at him and blink several times. I know he's playing. The cheeky smile is a dead giveaway. "I'm just saying, if I found out you accidently fell and your cock slipped inside her while you were playing naked Twister, well...let's just say you wouldn't have to worry about that kind of accident again."

"Let me get this straight. Naked Twister with Adele is fine, as long as I don't accidently slip and my dick doesn't land in one of her orifices?" My lips purse into a tight line. "No naked Twister then?"

"No naked Twister," I confirm.

"Well, you'll be happy to know that we haven't partaken in any naked games." He kisses my forehead. "I must admit, I like it when you're all possessive of me." He kisses me once again. "Where have you been?"

My entire posture stiffens with dread. "I'm working on something."

Ben releases me and scoots off the bed. He walks into the bathroom, and when he returns, he opens one of his drawers and slides on a pair of sweats. "What aren't you telling me?"

This isn't a conversation that can be had while I'm naked. I jump off the bed and start putting my clothes on. "It's complicated."

"Whatever it is, I just don't want you to leave again. We can make this work between us." He leans against the chest of drawers and crosses his arms in front of him.

"You're asking the impossible. Me being who I am would have your life in imminent danger, and not only would your life be in danger but anyone could take you and use you to get to me."

"I want us to be together."

I shake my head as I put my shoes on. "I can't see a way." Ben doesn't reply, and when I look up at him he's staring down at the floor. "What is it?" Is he hiding something from me?

"It's nothing." He pinches the bridge of his nose. "Where have you been?" he repeats in a darker tone.

"I can't tell you."

"Can't or won't?" I finish putting my shoes on and lean my elbows on my knees as I lower my chin. I hear Ben's long sigh. "I don't want to fight with you, Anna. I just want to be involved in your life and I want you to stay."

I push up off the bed and offer Ben the only thing I can—a smile. I place my hand to his warm, bare chest and tilt my head up to give him a kiss. "This is complicated," I repeat. I pull away and walk out of his bedroom.

"Let me make you something to eat," he says as he follows me down the hallway. "You can't leave yet."

I adore how cute he is, even though it's on the border of needy. I change direction and head into the kitchen. "Feed me. I'm hungry," I say as I make my way over to the barstools, pull one out, and sit.

A massive smile lights up Ben's face. He turns and jogs back to his room, and when he returns, he's wearing a black t-shirt. *What a shame.* Ben takes a packet of chicken out of the fridge along with some mushrooms and garlic. "So," he starts as he begins the preparations of dinner. "Something's going on and I'm not sure what it is."

"Is that a cryptic message I need to decipher?" I ask as I watch him.

"I mean at work."

Now this is interesting. "Like what?" I sit straighter, more attentive.

"Well, first of all that assassination of the married couple, and I feel like something's happening in and around Bankstown Creek." He shakes his head and sighs. "None of my contacts are talking but something appears to be happening from East Coast to the Midwest."

I have a feeling Katsuo is making a play to take over the area Ben's worried about. But I'm not going to know anything concrete until I go to this meeting with him. "What exactly are you worried about?"

"I need information, Anna. Do you by chance know anything about this?" He stops chopping and looks up at me.

"Maybe, but I won't know for sure until I go to a meeting."

"Meeting? What kind of meeting?" My jaw tenses with his question. "Oh." He nods once and resumes his chopping.

"I know this must be difficult for you, but all I ask is that you trust me."

"I do," he replies without hesitation.

"Then, you need to let me work."

"So it's work then? Not personal?"

I straighten in the seat and link my fingers together. "What do you mean?"

"The work you're doing, it's a mark, right? A hit?"

I clear my throat and look down at the food he's preparing. I've suddenly lost my appetite. "It is."

"A male hit?" Ben's voice is scratchy and tight.

"It is."

"And you have to get close to him?"

"I don't have to, but I choose to."

"Then just kill him and be done with it," he says with conviction.

"It's not that easy."

"Why?" he pushes. "If he's a paid target, why do you need to be close to him?" I swallow as I fidget where I sit. "Wait..." He places the knife down and stands taller. "Are you falling for him?"

"What?" I nearly shriek. "No way. He's..." I stop talking and shake my head.

"Then why can't you just kill him and move on? You could live here with me and we could have a life together."

I blink several times at Ben. "Live with you?"

"Why not?"

"I don't have the option to play happy family with you, Ben. There's no happily ever after for me. There's no family, no wedding, and no anything." I can feel myself becoming flustered. "That's never been in my future. Not since the day I was kidnapped and forged into the person I am today. I'll always be an assassin."

"We can..."

I hold my hand up to stop him. "Enough."

"Just tell me one thing."

If he mentions love or any of that fairy tale crap again, I'm going to lose my shit. "What?" I ask with a level of irritation.

"Are you sleeping with him?"

Well, that's a fucked question. I pull my shoulders back and lift my chin. "I'm doing what I have to do to get the information I need to protect..." I stop myself from finishing that loaded sentence.

"Protect what? Or who?"

I stand and take a step backward. "It doesn't matter." I look down at the food on the counter. "It looks good but I have to go."

"No, Anna, please," he calls after me as I head toward the door. "Don't go." I hear his footsteps quicken behind me. He grabs me by the upper arm and swings me around. "Please. I only just got you back."

Maybe I need to cool it with Ben, step away and let him heal from me. But I don't think I can do that. I hide behind my mask and give Ben a quick, yet false, smile. I cup his cheek and kiss his lips lightly. "I have to go, there are things I have to do."

"When will I see you again?"

"I'm not sure." Maybe never. I'm hurting him, and I hate that.

"Tomorrow."

"I can't."

"The next day." I shake my head. "When?"

"I'll be in touch." I easily shrug out of his loose grip and step backward. Why did I come here? I shouldn't have put him in this position. It's cruel and horrible of me to have done this. *Well, more cruel and horrible than normal.*

"Anna," he calls as I head out the front door.

I get in the car and pull out of the driveway as I watch him standing in the doorway of his house. "Fuck!" I yell and smash my hand on the wheel. "I'm such a fucking idiot."

I head to my house and park where Agent left the car for me. I sneak back into the house and grab a quick shower before I lie on the bed.

I shouldn't have gone.

But I can't find it in me to stay away. Not from Ben.

CHAPTER SIX

ANNA

Past

I lie in bed staring up at the ceiling after an exhausting day, tears leaking from my eyes. The image of Dad tied to the chair as Nox stood with a gun to his head, while Damon gave me the choice of leaving with them or Dad dying, constricts my throat.

Although I killed both Nox and Damon after they killed my father and blew up our house, I still can't help but feel guilty for what they did. If I wasn't so good at shooting a target, I wouldn't have sparked the interest of Ronan Murphy, and he wouldn't have sent his goons to kill my father and take me.

My life is a clusterfuck of complications. I can never return to Bankstown Creek because the memories I have are too painful to relive. I have to put all of that behind me and move on to my future.

The world I'm now in is so far removed from what I had with Dad. I had security and love from Dad, but now, I have a man I met a week ago by chance when I warned him about the imminent danger he was in. Here I am, in his industrial makeshift apartment where he's teaching me his ways of being an assassin.

I'm not sure this is something I can do. I'm fifteen and being taught how to be the ultimate killing machine. I wish I had Dad back.

A strangled sob gurgles at the base of my throat as I wipe the tears away. I miss him so much. I turn on my side. tuck my hands under my head, and try to close my eyes for sleep.

As I'm drifting, my skin tingles as a blanket of ice falls over me. My eyes spring open, and I turn just as Lucas sneaks into the room and jabs me with a cattle prod. "What the hell?" I yell as I shoot up out of bed.

"Training," he says and thrusts the cattle prod at me again. Bolts of electricity vibrate through my already drained body. "You have thirty seconds." He lunges at me with the prod again, but this time I jump back off my bed so he misses me. "Stupid move." I have essentially given myself no space to escape because I have the wall behind me.

My mind is spent from the training earlier, but I need to get out of here or he's going to continue jabbing me with the prod. He moves forward to hit me again, but I bring my elbow up and crack him in the face, giving me only a few seconds to escape the room and put distance between us. I make it out of the door to where his Porsche is parked inside the open, makeshift apartment. "I'm tired," I argue when he appears. I was hoping I had broken his nose, but I mustn't have hit him hard enough.

He comes at me with the long prod thrusting out in front of him. "Get over there." Lucas juts his chin behind me and I turn to see a table with two chairs and a black, blocky box sitting on the table, along with a bunch of wires.

"Shit," I whisper. He gets the drop on me and hits me again with the prod. "Stop that!"

"Polygraph testing."

"Lie detector?"

"Sit." He lifts the prod in a threatening way. I have a feeling I'm not going to escape that prod even if I do what he tells me. "This is something you may never need, but if you are ever caught by the police, this'll be the most valuable skill you'll ever master. Either way, you'll learn to beat the box right now." I look at the machine sitting on the table and nod once, though I get the feeling he wasn't asking, he was telling. "I'm going to strap you in." He walks around and begins to attach the straps all around me. Once finished, he sets the cattle prod aside and picks up a Taser.

"This is going to be hard, isn't it?"

"Yes, it'll be hard but this can save your life. The alternative is you end up dead or in jail."

"If I'm caught then maybe I deserve whatever comes to me." I look down at my thighs and shake my head.

Lucas tases me in the ribs making me double over in shocking pain. "Stop feeling sorry for yourself." I get my breath back and straighten. "Control your emotions or they will kill you." His tight jaw loosens and he takes a breath. "When you're strapped in, the person administering the test will need to establish a baseline so they can recognize true and false responses. You need to be completely in control of your body. Any little flicker will be picked up by the machine and then it'll be game over for you."

I lower my head and close my eyes for a moment. All the lessons Lucas has taught me have all required turning my emotions off and keeping a cool, level head. If I'm going to survive in this world, I'll need to bury my emotions, push any thought of my father away, and become a cold-blooded killer. I take several deep breaths to control myself.

"For every answer you give me that registers as false, I'll tase you."

I lift my head and stare at Lucas. "How comforting," I sarcastically snicker.

He slightly shakes his head. "This isn't meant to be comfortable. We're doing this to save your life."

I swallow the lump in my throat. "I know."

"First, a couple of questions to establish the baseline, you need to answer 'yes' to them."

I nod. "Okay."

"Is your name Anna Brookes?"

"Yes."

He marks the paper and looks up at me. "Are you fifteen years old?"

"Yes." He marks the paper again. What's he marking? How does someone read this? I should learn that too, so I can see what he's seeing.

Lucas grips the stun gun tightly in his left hand. I'm already dreading it, but I need to block that out and focus on my breath. "Is your name Jessica White?"

"Yes." Without warning he pokes the stun gun into my ribs, causing me to cry out in pain.

"Straighten up." I want to rub at the affected area, but instead, I close my eyes again and try to blank out any thoughts. Which, incidentally, is difficult when I'm being poked with electricity. "Is your name Fiona Lord?"

I don't even have a chance to reply when he tases me again. "Come on!" I groan.

"You won't be given an opportunity to screw this up. Imagine being captured by some drug dealer who will put a bullet in your head if you give one wrong answer." He stands and draws his gun from his waistband. "Would you prefer you work with a gun to your temple?" Lucas takes a step around the table and cocks his gun.

"No, I can do this," I say softly as I look at his gun, then lower my head. *Come on, pull yourself together.* Dad always taught me to breathe and focus. That's all I have to do. I have to breathe and focus. I can do this.

I just need to take myself to a place where everything is calm, where it's just me and a target on the range. I inhale a deep breath as my body calms with the sensation of complete peace.

"Is your name Anna Brookes?"

"No." I'm not tased.

"Is your name Jessica White?'

"Yes."

Lucas hits my thigh with the stun gun, keeping the contact with my leg slightly longer. An instant fire builds in my thigh, like it's been sawn in half with a blunt, burning saw. I hold onto the pain, keeping the hurt inside me. I refuse to give him the satisfaction of seeing how much this is killing me. He releases the taser and I straighten, daring him to give me more. I'm going to beat that damn machine, no matter how much he tases or prods me. "Is your name Anna Brookes?"

"No." He hits me again, the vibration of the electricity charging my fury.

"Is your name Fiona Lord?"

"Yes." The stun gun on my body causes me to shriek with pain. No, no, keep it together. You can do this.

"Is your name Anna Brookes?"

Something breaks inside of me. The pain is no longer even relevant. It's either this or death, and I'm not going to die, not because of some fucker who thinks they can outsmart me. My hair is clinging to my sweaty face, and my heart is beating so hard I can feel it thumping in my throat. Dad always taught me to breathe. *Get it together.* I inhale deeply through my nose and let the air pass through my pressed lips. I snap my eyes open and lift my head. "No," I say with confidence.

"Is your name Fiona Lord?"

"Yes."

"Are you fifteen?"

"No." The stun gun remains in his tight grip.

"Have you killed?"

"No." My body is in total submission to me. My breath is calm, my pulse is relaxed, my brain is laser focused.

"Is your hair blonde?"

Nope, brunette through and through. "Yes."

Lucas's brows lift in surprise. I'm going to beat this thing, and I don't care how many times he jabs me with the stun gun. "Would you kill me?"

"Yes."

He looks up and stares at me. "You would?"

"No," I reply and smirk.

He looks down again at the machine and scrunches his brows. "Training over." Lucas stands and begins to unstrap me from the machine. "Would you kill me?" he asks in a softer voice when he sits again.

"Of course not." I don't know. *Maybe.*

Once I'm out of the straps, I nurse the areas on my body where the stun gun remained for extended periods of time. "I didn't enjoy doing that," Lucas says as he sits again and glances at where I'm rubbing my hand.

"I know." I offer him a small smile.

Lucas stares at me for a moment before intaking a long breath. "There are three in total."

I slightly shake my head and lift my shoulders. "Three what?"

"You need to always be aware of your surroundings."

I purse my lips tight before dropping my hands into my lap. "I have no idea what you're talking about."

"There are three things regarding your surroundings that need to be top of mind and they're all men, and extremely dangerous. But, most of all, they're hungry enough to try and take each other out if they had the chance."

Ah, I see, he's warning me about other assassins. "Do you think they'll try and take me out?"

Lucas snorts with a dry chuckle. "I like how you said try."

I cock a brow. "Like I said, they can try."

"Your arrogance will get you killed, Anna."

"Nope. My arrogance is what's going to save me," I correct him with confidence.

The skin beneath Lucas's right eye trembles. I've been noticing he has small signs that tell me what he's thinking. The twitch beneath his eye means he's impressed. The smallest jerk of his pinky finger tells me when he's angry and trying to control his emotions. When he lifts his chin and juts it forward is the most telling. That's the one that tells me he's worried. Then I need to figure out if he's worried for me, or for himself. "Just remember, there are three," he quickly adds.

"I'm sure there's more."

"These three are the best in the field. They get paid the big bucks to take out the hardest targets."

"I can do it," I reply with confidence.

"Not yet you can't."

"Who are they?"

He lifts his chin and looks down his nose at me. "In time I'll tell you."

I suspect he's one of the three. Does this mean he's going to try and kill me? If so, why is he training me?

Time will tell. But for now, I'm going to soak up as much information as he can give me. There may be three top male assassins in the world, but all that is going to change.

In time.

CHAPTER SEVEN

— • —

ANNA

The knocking on the door wakes me from my sleep. It takes all of a few seconds for me to be up and out of bed with my Glock in my hand. I head toward the window and peek outside, making sure I'm not seen.

Fucking Katsuo.

His entourage of cars and men are all parked out the front. The night sky is broken by sun just breaking the horizon. I quickly hide my gun, mess my hair, and walk over to the door.

He bangs on it again.

"Who is it?" I call in a fake sleepy voice.

"Open up, Treasure." His voice causes my body to shiver from repulsion. But I don't have the luxury of showing my disgust in front of him.

I unlatch the door and open it. The moment I see him, I make sure my bright smile and wide eyes give him the reception he's expecting. I throw my arms around his neck and plant a kiss on his lips. The aroma of stale smoke and alcohol clings to his clothes. "I've missed you so much," I purr with enthusiasm.

He pushes back slightly and waltzes into my house. "Why didn't you pick up when I called earlier?" He gestures toward his men to look through my house.

I wrap my arms around my waist and step backward, putting on the air of innocence. "Did you call me?" I look around for my phone, knowing full well I let the battery die so I could use that excuse for this very reason. I look over to the kitchen counter where my phone is. I walk over and grab it. "Oh, the battery's dead," I say as I try to hit the power button. "Here." I hand it toward Katsuo and he snatches it out of my hand. "It's dead."

Katsuo tries to power it up and when it doesn't come to life, he throws it at the wall, where it smashes into pieces. "Do you think I'm an idiot?" *Is that rhetorical?*

"What? No, why?"

He takes a step closer toward me and I see his hands are balled into fists. I know what's about to happen, and although I can take him and his weak-ass excuse for security, I have to let this play out or I'll never know what he's doing in Bankstown Creek. He brings his hand back and slaps me hard across the face. This is his need to dominate and control. "You answer my calls, do you understand?"

"I can't, you broke my phone," I reply with a quiver to my voice.

He snaps his fingers and one of his men hands him a phone. "Make sure it's always charged and you answer my calls." He pushes the phone out toward me.

I cower away, giving him the thrill of domination he needs to let me into his life. I visibly swallow and blink back the pretend tears. Hesitantly, I reach out to take the phone. "I'm sorry," I whisper.

"Come here, Treasure." He wraps his hand around my wrist and pulls me into a tight embrace. "You make me crazy. You know that right? I was so worried about you that the moment I landed I came straight here."

"I know. I'm sorry."

"If anything would've happened to you..."

"But nothing did." I nestle into him and do my absolute best not to vomit all over him. He makes my stomach churn. But this will all be over soon.

"I've been thinking about something."

"What's that?"

He pulls back and laces his fingers through my bed hair and brings his lips down to mine. "Go have a shower because I don't like you looking like a homeless person." *I'm going to kick your fucking ass soon.* "We're going somewhere special."

Fucking finally! "Where are we going?"

"It's a surprise."

The meeting isn't until late tomorrow, though. Fuck, this isn't good. I bat my eyelashes at him and smile. "A little hint?" I place my palms together as if I'm praying and blink several times.

"It'll be fun." One of his men chuckles from beside him.

My skin crackles with electricity as I flick a quick glance over at the man who laughed. "Fun you say?" I ask as I lift my head to look at Katsuo. "If you say so."

"Wear something slutty."

"I have the slutty dress you asked me to buy. Do you want me to wear that?"

"No, that's for the meeting. Actually..." He casts a wandering eye over my body. "Go have a shower, and hurry up."

He's up to something, and whatever it is, it's either designed to catch me out or to give him satisfaction. If he tells me to screw one of his men while he watches, that's an automatic kill. It's bad enough I've had to have sex with *him*, I refuse to be passed around for his men's enjoyment. I'll end him, and I'll figure out another way to get the information I need about his interests and business in Bankstown Creek.

I head into the bedroom and quickly scan the room to make sure nothing of my true identity is showing. Of course, it isn't. This house has nothing of who I really am. It's a façade, a mask, a well-orchestrated front of what I want Katsuo to see.

I take a quick shower and when I head back into my room, Katsuo has laid out some clothes for me, and he's sitting on the edge of my unmade bed. With the towel wrapped around me, I look at the sundress, panties, and bra he's chosen for me to wear. I've never been a sundress kind of woman, but when I have to build an illusion of a normal woman, sundresses are a part of that normality. "Are we going for a picnic at stupid o'clock in the morning?" I ask as I eye the clothing.

"I think easy access is much more important in my choice of your wardrobe," he says with a leer. *Me killing you would be nice, too.*

"Easy access? Think you're going to get lucky, do you?" I tease as I bring my hand up to my cheek, where the skin is already darkening from that full-force slap he gave me not even half an hour ago.

"I said I was sorry," Katsuo groans half-heartedly. "What else do you want?"

"I didn't say anything," I reply, making sure I keep my cool.

"Get dressed."

"Are you going to leave so I can?" He intakes a sharp breath and leans back on the bed, propping himself up with one elbow as he scans my body. "Alright then." I drop the towel and dress in front of him, teasing as I step into my panties and seductively draw them up my legs. I keep eye contact with Katsuo as I tempt him with my body and confidence. I have no shame in using my body if it means I'll get the information I need quicker.

"If we had time, I'd bend you over this bed right now."

Thankfully my back is turned to him so he can't see my visceral reaction. If I could, I'd vomit on him before killing him. All I can do is visualize the delicious ways I'll torture him. Maybe I'll use my drill with a long bit and drive it through his skull slowly. Or, maybe I'll scalp him while I have him tied to a table. Or, perhaps I'll have him up on his tiptoes suspended by a barbed wire noose and when his toes cramp and he drops from tiptoes, the barbed wire will tighten around his neck. The possibilities are delicious.

I turn and flutter my eyelids. "What a shame." I lift one shoulder and waltz out of the bedroom. I'm greeted with the beefy back of one of his men. What an idiot. He's standing rigid as he protects his boss from any dangers outside of the room. If only he knew the danger is *inside* the room. *Fool.*

"In such a hurry for your surprise." Katsuo snickers with an erect posture and high shoulders. His confidence should be unnerving, but to me this means it's going to be fun. He stands and grips my hand as he wooshes past me. "Then let's get this party started." I couldn't have said it better myself.

His car pulls up to an industrial area that appears to be deserted. The area is a good half hour from Bankstown Creek, and quite isolated. "Where are we?" I ask with a fake tinge of worry. I know his men are carrying, and I only need to get to one of them, disarm him, and put them all down before anyone realizes what's hit them.

"You're coming to an important meeting, and it got me thinking that I really don't know much about you. Your background check doesn't show a lot and that has me…" He thins his lips and jovially tilts his head from side to side. "…perplexed."

"Perplexed?" I ask as I furrow my brows. My acting skills are out of this world, I should win an Academy Award for my fake innocence. I stare at him. "I thought we've been over this."

"There are a lot of powerful people coming, and I need to make sure you're who you say you are."

Internally, I'm giving myself high fives. I know exactly why he's brought me here. In all my years, I've never been given a polygraph, and in this moment, I'm thankful to Lucas for teaching me how to beat the box. I tug at the sundress I'm wearing and wring the material through my fingers. "What are we doing here?" I ask in a particularly vulnerable and frightened voice.

"My sweet Treasure." *Balk.* "If you do well here, then you'll have my absolute trust until the day I die." Which will be sooner than you think. "But, make no mistake." His man steps forward and hands him a Glock. "If you don't do well, then…" He peers down to the gun, then back to me.

Game on. My eyes widen and I take a small step back as I gulp. The hand of one of his men falls to my lower back and he pushes me forward, like I'm cattle. Fucker will lose his hand if he touches me again. "Um." I can't appear confident or he's going to know something is wrong. I hate playing this role, but it's part of the job.

Katsuo steps toward me and links our fingers together before beginning to drag me toward the open door of one of the buildings. "Don't be scared."

"You just told me if I don't pass some kind of stupid test that you're going to kill me. How can I *not* be scared?"

"It would be difficult for me to actually do it."

Fucking psycho. But at least we're playing *my* game. I pull my shoulders back and shake my head. "If this is what I have to do for you to trust me, then let's get on with it."

We walk through the door and down a small corridor before we emerge into a massive room. It's like a scene out of a horror movie. Only some lights are working, while there's maybe twenty of his men standing along the walls watching. Wow, twenty of them for little ol' me. *How cute.* Like they'd stand a chance. In the center of the room is a table with three chairs, two on one side, and one on the other. I can't help but smile internally. This is exactly what I thought was going to happen. Thankfully, on the car ride out I was able to use the guise of worry to calm myself.

"Do you know what this is?" Katsuo asks, leading me over to the table.

I feign worry and look around the room as I maintain my veneer of vulnerability and innocence. "Um, it's a lie detector. I've seen them in movies."

Lucas put me through hell learning how to beat the lie detector. And for that, I'm eternally grateful to him. "It's a polygraph. It's designed to read you and tell if you're lying."

I continue with my ruse as I cower into myself and step backward. "I'm...I'm..." I swallow and look around the room again. All his men appear unfazed by my obviously upset nature. I wonder how many women have died because of this stupid test. "I'm scared."

"If you have nothing to hide, you shouldn't be frightened. Now, this machine is one hundred percent accurate."

No, dumbass, it's not. "Are you sure I have to do this?" I try to take yet another step backward as I look for any of the exits in a pretense of fear.

"Shhh, Treasure. It's okay." He gently pulls me back toward the table and sits me down. "Just tell the truth." He leans into me and places a kiss to my forehead. He walks over to the other side of the machine and sits in one of the two chairs. He nods and indicates for someone to come over.

A man with a cigarette hanging out of his mouth strolls over and begins to strap me up to the machine. His ash falls on my leg as he finishes. "You don't have to do this," I beg as my voice trembles with panic.

"This will all be over soon. And then, we'll put it behind us and you'll have my undying trust." The smoking operator puts out his cigarette and takes another out of the pack and lights it. "We're good to start whenever you're ready," Katsuo instructs him.

"Please, no," I futilely beg one last time.

"Answer only yes or no to the questions I ask. I'll ask you two questions to establish the baseline for the rest of the examination. Please answer yes to both of them." I take a moment to calm my heart, my mind, and my body. "Is your name Anna Moore."

Technically no. "Yes." He marks the paper as his cigarette hangs out of his mouth.

"Do you own a green SUV?"

Not a green one. "Yes."

The operator marks the paper again and looks over to Katsuo. He indicates that the detector has registered the responses he's looking for and that they're ready to commence the interview.

"Are you a government agent?" Interesting; the operator has done this many times before because he's not reading from anything.

"No."

"Are you a law enforcement officer?"

I want to laugh at his ridiculous question, but I have to maintain my mask and my cover. "No."

"Are you from a rival family?"

"No."

"Did you meet Katsuo Vang by chance?"

"Yes."

"Are you attracted to Katsuo Vang?"

I look at Katsuo and try to muster a smile. "Yes." *Liar.*

"Are you trying to acquire information on Katsuo Vang?"

"No." *Yes.*

"Do you have any siblings?"

"No."

"Have you been sexually active with anyone other than Katsuo Vang since you met?"

Hell yeah, with Ben. Mmmm, Ben. "No."

"Do you own a weapon?"

Presumptuous of him to think I only have one. "No." *Not a weapon; I own an arsenal of weapons.*

"Are you attracted to Katsuo Vang?"

Has he got vanity issues? "Yes."

"Are you after Katsuo Vang's money?"

This one actually makes me snicker aloud. "No." His money? I couldn't care less about his money.

The operator takes a long drag of his cigarette before pushing the butt out with his tongue and letting it fall to the floor. "Do you have any other questions, Mr. Vang?"

Katsuo turns and flicks his gaze toward the operator. The operator stands and walks around to take all the straps off me. He then places a hand to Katsuo's shoulder and gives him a knowing nod. Katsuo sits back in his chair and links his fingers together. The air is thick with tension as I pretend to worry about my results. I keep darting glances between Katsuo, his men, and the exit. "At the meeting, you'll be seen but not heard, understand?"

I let out a long, relieved sigh and clasp at my chest. "You had me worried."

"I had to make sure you're who you said you were. It's refreshing to see you're not after my money."

"Money isn't a driving factor for me." Not when it comes to protecting Ben from you.

"Now, the other thing we need to discuss, and it's not up for negotiations, is your safety."

"My safety? Am I not safe with you?" I glance at his crew.

"Treasure, you're always safe with me. It's the outside world I'm concerned about. So, I'll be assigning you a complete security detail."

Well, this is going to make it harder to see Ben. "A security detail?" I ask in a calm voice. "More than the car that sits outside my house?"

"I need to know where you are at all times, Anna. You'll be selling your house, moving in with me, and closing down your business. You no longer need it. I'll be taking care of anything you need. If you require something, just ask me for it and I'll make sure you get it," he says casually.

"Wow, so that's a no from me."

"I told you it's not up for negotiations. I'm not asking, I'm telling you how things are going to be from here on in."

I stand from the chair and begin walking away. Katsuo is on his feet and following me, while barking orders to his men in Japanese. "Where are you going?" He catches up and stands in front of me.

"I just sat there and let your man interrogate me." I point toward the middle of the room. "I've played by your rules without question. But demanding I move in with you and stop working? That's a hard 'no' from me. I've worked long and hard to build my business. I barely know you, and I'm not ready for that kind of commitment to or from you. And as far as I'm concerned, not working is a 'no.' I refuse to rely on anybody for anything." I cross my arms in front of my chest for dramatic effect.

"I told you, it's the way things are going to be moving forward."

"Fine, then take me back to my house." I lift my chin.

"Good, I'm glad you've come to your senses."

"I have. Once I'm back there, don't contact me again."

"Anna," he growls. "Stop acting like a child."

"Stop treating me like one." He takes a step forward, and I counter by moving backward. "I'm not giving up my freedom," I say firmly.

"Your freedom? You'll have financial freedom, which means you won't want for anything ever again."

I shake my head. "No. I don't want to be dependent on you, Katsuo. If that's what you want, then I'm sorry, I'm out." *Come on, yield to me.*

He lowers his chin and runs his hand through his hair. "I'll make you a deal."

You tell me what I want to know and I kill you now? "What?" I ask with obvious distaste.

"You can keep your little job for now." Condescending ass.

"And my house."

"No, you move in with me today."

I turn my mouth down, shrug, and continue to move past him. "I've been accommodating, but I refuse to lose any part of me because you want to control me."

"Fine," he relinquishes. *Yes.* "You can keep your house, but I install cameras and one of the rooms is used for my men."

Fuck. The security cameras will be easy for Agent to get around. The man in the room won't be. I have to play on his paranoia and his need to own me. I step closer and glance around the room. "I'm not comfortable with anyone in my house, especially if I don't know them. I'm happy to have them outside, but not inside."

He runs his hand through his hair again. *Yes, I've got him.* "I'll agree to this on one condition."

"Which is?"

"In one month, you move in with me." I open my mouth to argue but he shushes me. "You can keep your job, but you have to move in. If you want me to agree with your conditions then you have to agree with mine. We'll compromise."

Not that this is a real relationship. If it was, then he'd move me in and slowly isolate me until I'm completely reliant on him. "Six months." I'll have all the information I need soon and he'll be dead, but I have to make this look real.

"Two months."

"One year," I counter and lift a brow cockily.

"Four months and that's it. You have no other options."

Buddy, I have plenty of options, including putting a bullet between your eyes. "Terms accepted," I say and give him a small smile.

"Good." He moves in to kiss me and with all the confidence in the world, I return the kiss.

Now, I need to wait for this damned meeting tomorrow night and figure out what the fuck is actually going on so I can take care of it. Once and for all.

CHAPTER EIGHT

— • —

ANNA

"What have you got here that I can use for a listening device?" I ask Agent as I pace back and forth, keeping an eye on the cars outside my house. "I need you to be able to hear what's happening tonight so you can run backgrounds on everyone."

"I don't have anything, 15. Only weapons. It needed to be clean in case he swept it."

"Fuck," I grumble. I take my earpiece out and sit on the edge of the bed. I'll make it work.

I see Katsuo's car approach and pull up out in front of my house. A bodyguard exits the car and opens the back door for him. Another car pulls up behind his and yet another one of his men rushes to walk behind Katsuo while keeping a careful eye around the sleepy neighborhood. The door opens and Katsuo enters my house. I rush out of the bedroom, pretending to be startled. "What are you doing here?" I ask as I throw my arms around his neck and hug him. God, I can't wait until I no longer have to pretend with him.

"I was thinking."

"Could be dangerous," I add and give him a small cheeky wink.

"You have no idea how dangerous I am, Treasure," he replies. Is he trying to inflate his own ego?

"You're like a big, giant, squishy marshmallow," I say and lean in to kiss his lips. Ugh, the taste of cigarette smoke mixed with alcohol lingers on his mouth. It's not sexy, not on him.

He smacks my butt and kisses my forehead. "This is Tyler."

A taller guy steps forward and extends his hand to me. "Ma'am."

I step back from Katsuo and reach for Tyler's hand. My skin pebbles, expecting that familiar serpent-bite sting as I wrap my fingers around his hand. But it doesn't happen. Tyler isn't evil, not like the rest of Katsuo's crew. Hmmm, interesting. "It's Anna," I correct. "Ma'am makes me sound old, and I'm not that old."

Tyler's cheeks turn pink as he lowers his chin. "No, ma'am, you're certainly not."

Instantly Katsuo squares his shoulders as he turns to Tyler. "Tyler is your new bodyguard." *Seriously?* I'm sure I could disarm Tyler in two seconds flat. Maybe I need to be Tyler's bodyguard. "He'll go everywhere you go." *Great.* "I was thinking about the dress you bought for the meeting, and I don't want you in that. You're too precious to show off in a slutty dress. You need class." He cocks a brow at me. I need class? You need a bullet, that's what you need, *asshole.*

"What have you got in mind?"

"Tyler's taking you to Prada."

Prada is a good hour away. "Is he?" I flash a look over to Tyler. Maybe this is a good thing; I'll be able to suss him out. Katsuo turns to Tyler and puffs out his chest. "If anything happens to Anna..." he threatens ominously. Is he going to finish the threat?

"I understand, sir," Tyler replies.

"Don't let her out of your sight." He lifts his finger to menacingly point at Tyler. "If anything happens..." Seriously, enough with the half threats. Katsuo turns to me and smashes his mouth to mine. I hate kissing him, despise it. But it's something I have to do. *For now.* "I'll see you at the meeting." He waggles his brows suggestively as he skims his eyes down over my body. *Yuck.* He glances at Tyler and scowls once more before heading back out to his car.

Tyler straightens and lifts his chin as he stands stoically just inside the entrance to my house. "I guess you're taking me to Prada."

"Yes, ma'am."

I suck in an annoyed breath with this whole *ma'am* business and slightly shake my head. Without saying another word, I return to the bedroom to get ready. I hate how Katsuo thinks I need to be a kept woman. But then again, it's a small sacrifice in the grander scheme of things. I have to suck it up.

The ride to Prada is tensely silent. Tyler's eyes nervously dart everywhere while he's driving. He's not cocky or arrogant, more like cautious, as if he's expecting the worst to happen.

I'm not one to generally make small talk, especially when it's not with a target I'm attempting to infiltrate. Tyler doesn't pose a threat to me, although there's something about him. He doesn't give me those deathly creeps Katsuo and his men do. "How long have you worked for Katsuo?"

"Long enough," he replies is a cold, emotionless drawl.

"That long?" I lift my brows and look out the window. "Do you know who I am?"

"Mr. Vang's companion."

"Do you know anything else about me?"

"No, ma'am." His shoulders pull back in the smallest way as he glances at me from the rearview mirror. He's lying. He knows something. I need to know who he is. Maybe he's been sent in from a rival to infiltrate and learn the inner workings of Katsuo's empire. *You and me both, buddy.* Only difference is, I want to tear him down to keep Ben and Bankstown Creek safe.

"Tell me about yourself, Tyler," I say trying to tease any information I can get from him. "Where did you work before Mr. Vang?"

"Places."

"Places? Any I'd know of?"

"No."

"Man of many words."

"Miss Moore, if you don't mind, I don't like small talk." The corner of my mouth drags up into a smirk. That's his way of saying I'm not talking to you because I might say something I shouldn't. I'm careful to not make my interest obvious as I watch him watch me. Half an hour goes by when he finally says, "If you don't mind me saying, you're not like the others."

The others? "What do you mean?"

"You're not the usual type Mr. Vang prefers."

"No? How so?"

"He prefers for them to be..." He clears his throat and pulls at the stiff collar of his dress shirt. "...dumber," he finally says.

"Dumber?"

"They like spending his money and talking loudly on their phone while looking at their nails."

"Do you stereotype everyone, or are you just a misogynist by nature?"

"I didn't mean to offend you," he quickly adds. "I was trying to point out how you're not his usual type. He usually prefers girls who are more self-absorbed than you are."

He has no idea how wrong that sentence is. "Girls? As in underaged?" I challenge with sarcasm.

"I mean women."

"Hmmm." Thought so. "Self-absorbed? So now you're saying I don't take care of myself?"

"I think I'm going to shut up now."

"I think you better explain yourself before you do shut up."

"Miss Moore, I only meant that since I've worked for Mr. Vang, he's never dated anyone. He's had plenty of *women* he uses as arm candy, but he's never dated anyone like you in the past."

Now we're getting somewhere. "There's *no one* like me, Tyler."

He flicks his gaze up to look in the mirror and smiles. "I don't doubt that, Miss Moore." What does he know? Am I going to have to take him down too? My gut is telling me he's a friendly and not a threat. With disregard for the road rules, Tyler navigates the roads like there's no one else on them.

The rest of the drive to Prada is shrouded in silence. He pulls up in front of the store, and I reach for the handle. "I'll do that," he says. "Wait in the car, Miss Moore."

He's out of the car before I have a moment to voice my opinion. I hate being treated like a china doll. I'm fearless, and I can handle anything that comes at me. Including an overzealous bodyguard who's hiding something. He opens the door and I sit looking up at him from beneath my lashes. "Oh, I can come out now, can I?" My sarcasm is heavy.

He holds his hand out for me to take. I wave it away and slide out of the car easily. "I should've known," he mumbles under his breath.

I shake my head as I step in front of him. *Smart-ass.* I like that. "Should we run inside in case the baddies are watching me? Maybe they'll storm Prada and take me hostage." I can't contain my grin.

He clears his throat and slams the car door shut. "This way, Miss Moore," he gestures as he walks ahead and opens the door to Prada.

The storefront itself is simple and elegant. The carpet beneath my shoes is luxurious and the walls are crisp white with high quality artwork of their products hanging tactfully. There are crystal clear glass shelves without a speck of dust on them that hold a few styles of handbags. Again, nothing is over the top and gaudy, more like pristine and rich. It really oozes wealth and opulence.

An older woman who's absolutely stunning approaches with a wide smile. Her hair is impeccable as it falls over her shoulders and her makeup is flawless. "Welcome to Prada. My name is Sissy. May I offer you a beverage?"

"Thank you, Sissy—" I start but Tyler interrupts.

"Mr. Vang called ahead."

"Of course." She smiles between Tyler and me. "Miss Moore if you'd like to take a seat, I'll inform your personal shopper you're here." She heads toward the door and locks it.

"You're locking the door?" I ask as I carefully assess the store.

"Mr. Vang's instructions," she offers with a kind smile. *Really?* He made them close the store for me? What a control freak. "He asked that we make your visit comfortable and that your safety is of utmost importance."

He has some serious issues going on. "Thank you."

"Miss Moore?" I look over toward a man who looks damned good. He's dressed in a fine suit and smells like a refreshing breeze coming off of the ocean. "My name is Kyle. Mr. Vang said we're looking for a dress?"

"Apparently so."

"May I?" He extends his hand to help me up from the comfortable sofa. When I reach for it, I feel nothing. Kyle is simply someone who works here and not an enemy. "Damn, you have hips," he says with a smile. "I like a woman who has an hourglass figure."

I look down at my body, then back to Kyle. "Well, I like the way I look, too."

"Good, so you should. Now, when we're looking for an ensemble, we start with the shoe and work our way up. Let's head over to our shoes." He glances at my face where his eyes land on the bruise for a moment too long. He flicks a look over to Tyler, then back to me before we begin to make our way toward the back of the store. Tyler moves to follow us, but Kyle holds his hand up. "It's best you stay here."

"I'm to stay with Miss Moore," Tyler insists.

"I'll be fine." I smile softly to Tyler. "Besides, Katsuo wouldn't want you looking at me while I'm trying on dresses."

Tyler slightly extends his neck and peers at the car, parked illegally out in front of the Prada store. He turns and positions himself just inside the door, making sure no one enters the store.

"Shall we?" Kyle asks.

"Lead the way."

Kyle leads me down a spacious, brightly-lit corridor that opens into another open area with two more sofas and four private fitting rooms. Kyle peeks over my shoulder to make sure Tyler isn't following us. "We can get you out," he whispers.

"Sorry?"

He looks at my bruise again. "We can get you out," he repeats. "We can help you. You can't stay with someone who does that to you."

Kyle has a heart of gold. "This." I lift my hand to lightly touch the bruise. "Is handled." I cock a brow as I wink at him. "You have nothing to worry about with me. But I thank you on behalf of women who aren't able to help themselves. Trust me, Kyle, I'm good."

He chews on the inside of his cheek and finally gives me a small nod. "If you ever need help..."

"Thank you." I rub my hand up and down his arm. If only he knew the torture I can inflict on a person.

Kyle steps back and claps his hands together once. "Okay then. Now, shoes. High? Stiletto? Pumps? What are you most comfortable with?" Kyle looks around and snickers. "I mean, a stiletto could make for a good weapon."

I can't help but chuckle. "They have in the past," I say. This stops Kyle's snicker dead, and he stares at me with wide eyes and a gaping mouth. "I'm joking." His shoulders instantly relax. *Although, I'm not.*

He turns again and waves his hand to indicate the racks of shoes. "Now, what do you like to wear?"

Practical and comfortable. Something I can run in, something with a steel tip so I can enforce maximum damage. "Nothing overly high. A small heel."

"Small for you and small for me could be very different. What are we talking, five-inch heel?"

"Two or three would be the maximum."

"That's a good start. Do you have a color preference for the dress?"

"Let's go with something conservative, maybe a solid color?"

"Black? Black pairs with everything."

"Black is good."

"You're an easy client. I like you." The next hour is spent trying on only a few pairs of shoes and no more than five dresses. I end up settling on a black, thigh-length, fitted dress that shows off my curves perfectly, paired with pumps. Thankfully Kyle made the experience a lot less torturous than what I was expecting.

Kyle carries the boxes toward the front of the store. "I must say, you made this a painless experience," I tell him.

"Thank you." He smiles with genuine affection.

The sound of a screeching car raises the hair on the back of my neck to attention. My skin erupts into goose bumps as I turn to see what's going on. The hypnotic sound of guns shooting causes my stomach to ripple with excitement. "Get down!" Tyler runs toward me and throws himself over my body.

The force of his tackle propels me forward causing me to smash my head on the glass display case. Tyler's entire body is sheltering me. The sound of the shots is coming from outside the store, but Tyler isn't taking any chances.

Funny thing is, he's not behaving like security. The way he's using his body over mine to shield me gives me presidential-protection-detail vibes. "Stay down," he whispers in my ear as I try to buck him off me.

I know Tyler is carrying and if I can get to his gun, I can protect all of us. "Let me up."

He pushes his body further into mine. "I said stay down," he repeats with a guttural roar.

The gunfire continues from up the street and within seconds, there are various sirens coming in from every direction. I don't think this was a targeted attack, more like some lunatic opening fire on innocent people. Don't get me wrong, I'm all for killing people, but not innocents. They deserve protecting. *Well, most of them.* With some, it doesn't matter what happens to them.

Tyler stays on top of me, protecting my body with his for at least another minute. I can hear shouting and cars screeching away. The police must be following the person who opened fire. "Are you okay?" Tyler's body becomes lighter as he slowly stands. "Stay down while I assess the situation."

Assess the situation? Those are quite technical words coming from someone who's personal security for a dick I'll be killing soon. I really hope Tyler doesn't stand in my way when it comes to killing Katsuo. Tyler hasn't done anything to me and I don't *want* to kill him, but I will if he tries to protect Katsuo.

I stand, ignoring Tyler's pleas. "Miss Moore, I told you to..." He takes a breath and rushes toward me. "We need to get you to the hospital."

Suddenly my vision blurs and a pounding headache develops over my right eye. I lift my hand to feel where the throbbing is coming from. My fingers touch something warm, thick, and wet. I lower my hand to see blood on my fingertips. I know what this means. I've got a damn concussion. My knees weaken and I stumble forward. Tyler leaps forward to catch me. "It's just a little cut. I'll be..." *Fuck.*

I blink several times, trying to focus as I ineffectually swat at the gentle touch on my cheek. "There's my Treasure."

"What happened?" I ask as I attempt to sit up.

"Please, don't get up, Anna," a female voice says. My attempt to focus is slow, so I keep blinking until I can finally see. Katsuo is sitting beside me, carefully watching me, while an older lady is hovering over a medical bag. "How are you feeling?" I know exactly where we are. We're in his penthouse suite. I hate this bedroom.

"Treasure, are you okay?"

God, he irritates me. "I'm okay." I lift my hand to feel for the gash but it's been covered up.

"Miss Moore, my name is Doctor Vivian Hall. Can you tell me what day it is today?" She walks over toward me and stands beside Katsuo. "Mr. Vang, I need to see to my patient." She cocks a brow at him impatiently.

Katsuo's nostrils flare as he glares at her. What a possessive dick. I could lean forward, pretend to kiss him, wrap my arm around his neck and squeeze until he has no more life left. There's no one here to protect him, other than the doc, who'd probably do everything in her power to bring him back to life. She's done nothing to me, so I'm not keen on killing her for doing her job. *Ugh.* "Katsuo, please." I place my hand on his upper arm and gently pet in circular motions. "I know you're worried but Doctor Hall is trying to do her job." I add a small smile to soften the impact.

He runs his tongue over his teeth and snaps a fierce scowl at the doctor. "You have ten minutes." Standing, he walks out of the room.

There's a line between caring and asshole. He's gone way over to the asshole side. "Anna, can you tell me what day it is today?" the doctor asks. Once I answer, I touch at my wound again. "You had a gash on your head, so I closed it off."

"Stitches?" I ask disgusted.

"No, I managed to close it with glue. You'll have a small scar but nothing noticeable." She sits on the side bed and shines her flashlight into my eyes. "Can you tell me what happened?"

"Where's Tyler?"

"Who?"

She places the small flashlight on the bed and starts feeling at my neck. "Tyler?"

"I wasn't brought here for whoever this Tyler man is. My instructions from Mr. Vang are to make sure you're okay." Her hands are warm as she continues her examination of me. Shit, where's Tyler? "You have a concussion, which is what caused you to black out. I'll be advising Mr. Vang that you need to be monitored for the next twenty-four hours. I'll leave instructions for him." Yeah, yeah, I know. If I start vomiting or blacking out, I need to go to the hospital. Been there, done that. She looks down at her tablet where she's making notes and says, "You do have bruising around your eye that doesn't look like it happened today."

Damn it, now I have to lie to her. "I was elbowed in the face."

"Did you run into the elbow or did the elbow run into your face?" she asks in a softer, more caring tone. A few seconds of silence pass between us. She glances at the door and shifts to sit closer to me. "If you need help." She's the second person today who's offered. I like how not everyone in Katsuo's orbit falls to their knees for him. And to think, I was contemplating killing her only a few moments ago. I mean, I wouldn't have felt good about it, but I absolutely would've done it if I had to. *For the greater good.*

I give her a small smile. "Thank you for your help today, Doctor Hall."

Her shoulders droop as she releases a breath. I've dampened her silent offer of help, but she also has no idea that I have other plans for Katsuo. She finally stands and returns to her doctor's bag, places her tablet into it, and closes it. Doctor Hall hesitates for a moment before turning and offering a professional smile. "Please, take care of yourself."

"I will, thank you."

The moment her hand is about to reach the door knob, Katsuo bursts in. "I was coming to find you, Mr. Vang. Miss Moore has a concussion, and she'll need to be carefully monitored for the next twenty-four hours. If she begins to vomit, has double vision, severe headaches, or blacks out again, you'll need to take her to the hospital right away."

Katsuo waves her away like she's a fly on shit. Well, I guess that's what she is, to him. *Shit.* She turns and offers me one more silent offer of help. I ignore her and turn my *fake* loving attention to Katsuo. "I was so scared," I say playing on the damsel in distress aspect.

"Treasure, I was so worried about you." He wraps his arms around me and trails kisses from my cheek down my neck. Katsuo pulls back and stares at me. "I'll have a few of my men watching you when I leave."

"Wait, what? Aren't I coming to the meeting with you?"

"You have a concussion. You need to stay home and rest."

"I didn't go through all of this to stay home. You need to have me there, don't you?"

"I don't *need* you, no." His jaw tenses as he pulls his shoulders back.

"Oh." I lower my chin and downturn my lips. "I thought you wanted me to be there so you could maybe show everyone how we're together." I swallow as I try my hardest to cry. Damn it, the tears aren't coming, but I need to change the trajectory of this conversation. "I guess maybe I don't mean as much to you as you do to me."

His arms going immediately around me tells me I'm in for this fucking meeting. "Of course, you do. If you think you'll be okay to come."

"No one is going to care for me like you do, Katsuo," I say as I pull back and stare into his evil-as-fuck, hard eyes. "No one," I emphasize.

"You're right." He puffs his chest out with arrogance. "You're coming," he says with resolve. *Duh, I know.* It was my idea to start with. "Until the meeting, I'll have one of my men stay with you."

"Where's Tyler?" I ask. I still need to figure out who he is.

"I'll deal with him."

"What do you mean by that?"

"You were hurt, he knows what the consequences are." He stands and buttons his suit. "I'll be assigning someone new to you."

Fuck, he's going to kill Tyler. Truth be told, I'm all for killing. Hell, it's how I've made all my money. But killing him because he was doing what Katsuo told him to do, doesn't sit well with me. "Tyler protected me, and I trust him."

Katsuo's lips thin as he tilts his head to the side. "You were hurt."

"Because of what Tyler did, I'm alive. He threw himself on me to protect me. He used his body as a human shield to protect someone he met just this morning. If you do anything to Tyler then..." I shake my head and gaze off to the side. "I can't believe you'd hurt someone who used their body to protect me. I'd rather have him than anyone else you've assigned to me." Besides, I can slip past Tyler to go see Ben when I need to.

"Are you attracted to Tyler?" Is he serious? Katsuo roughly grips my chin and yanks my face toward him. "I asked if you're attracted to him?" He lowers his face level with mine. "Answer me." Angry spittle flies from his mouth as his fingers dig into my face.

"No. of course not. Put me on that stupid lie detector if you don't believe me."

He immediately releases my chin and wraps me in his arms. "I know, baby, I know." Fucking crazy-ass psycho. "You make me so jealous. If only you wouldn't ask about other men."

"I trust him," I say as I wrap my arms around him. "He showed me he'd do anything to protect me, so in my eyes, who else better to be assigned to me? I mean, if that doesn't prove to you how good he is, then what will?" I feel him tense in my arms. God, I hate having to baby him and inflate his sensitive ego. "Other than you, I don't trust anyone else to look after me." Insert internal eye roll.

He kisses my forehead before releasing me from his grip. "I'd kill for you, Anna."

As opposed to me biding my time until I kill him. "I like how I feel when I'm with you." Jesus, can I be any more corny?

"Go have a shower and rest, the meeting tonight will be intense."

Oh, it will? My skin covers in goose bumps again, this time from excitement. Now we're talking my language.

CHAPTER NINE

ANNA

After a lengthy shower, I need to get myself ready for the meeting. As I walk out of the bathroom with a towel wrapped around my body, I can hear a muffled voice. The voice is hushed, and I can instantly tell it's not Katsuo because his voice booms with an over-the-top arrogance. The low voice is coming from just outside the bedroom. The door is closed, so I place my ear to it in an attempt to hear what's being said. It's broken and I'm only picking up a few words. "No, sir." A small pause. "She..." She what? "...kill me." Another pause. "Requested me?" What? I hate not knowing what's said. "Check in." Check in? "Yes, sir." It's clear Tyler's talking to someone, but I can't quite figure out who.

Time to make my presence known. I open the door with only a towel wrapped around my body and one around my hair. I scan the hallway to see who Tyler's talking to. His eyes instantly land on my legs as he drags his gaze up my towel-covered body. "I'll see you when I get home, sweetheart," he says in his normal speaking voice.

Sweetheart my ass. Now I know he's lying about something. The conversation doesn't go from whispers and "sirs" to normal and "sweetheart" unless you're attempting to hide something. "Tyler," I say as I step back, pretending he's startled me.

"I'm sorry, Miss Moore, I thought you were in the shower."

"Well, I was, but I was coming out to find Katsuo. But, now I have you. Maybe you can answer my question."

"Which is what?" he replies as he shoves his phone in his pocket and turns his back to me so he doesn't have to keep looking at my towel-clad body.

"In the confusion of what happened earlier, did we end up getting the clothes from Prada?"

"Um. Yes, they were delivered about an hour ago. They're hanging in the closet. Do you think it's a good idea that you go anywhere tonight?"

"There's no place I'd rather be." I close the door and head over to the closet to get ready for this meeting. Finally, my patience will be rewarded.

I double-check myself in the mirror before heading out to find Katsuo. He's in his office, drinking a scotch as he sits back in his chair, looking at something on his computer. "Hey," I say as I walk over and sit on the edge of his desk, giving me the best view of what's on his computer. I only manage to catch a few graphs before he clicks out of it and goes into screen saver.

"You look beautiful." He turns in his chair, stands, and pushes my legs open so he can snugly fit between them. "I'd like to tear this dress off you." He lowers his face to take my mouth.

"Nope." I turn my head. "Lipstick."

"That's a beautiful shade. It would like good around the base of my cock."

Not in this lifetime, buddy. "And ruin my dress?" I bat my eyelashes. I lean in closer and whisper, "If you're a good boy, maybe when we return." Hopefully I can load him up with alcohol and escape having to do anything like that with him. *Blech.*

Katsuo takes in a sharp breath and collapses back into his seat as he stares at me. "I've never had anyone say 'no' to me before."

I lift my shoulder slightly and stand from the corner of the desk. "Then date one of them." I sharply turn and begin to walk out of his office, making sure to sway my hips, knowing he's staring at me.

"Damn woman, I could watch your ass all day." I hold back the eye roll. "But we need to leave. Are you ready to go?" If only I could bring my trusty guns with me. Unfortunately, I have nowhere to hide them, and I'm not ready to give away my identity yet.

"Do you think I'm ready?" I casually flick my hand over my shoulder. "I'm going to the kitchen for a cocktail. When you decide you're ready to go, that's where you'll find me." Playing hard to get is easy with Katsuo. I know he's going to be up and out of that chair in seconds. Sure enough, I hear the scrape of the chair against the floor.

"Wait." Like putty in my hands.

I stop and turn to wait for him. Katsuo is shrugging into his suit jacket, then checks his pockets. "There's a protocol for these meetings that the wives and girlfriends are expected to adhere to."

"Such as?"

"You'll sit in the allocated seat behind me." How subservient of you. "You're not permitted to talk with the exception of asking to go to the bathroom or to address the waitstaff." Wow, how authoritarian of him. "We'll be meeting with heads of other factions and you'll see that their wives and or girlfriends aren't permitted to sit at the table with them either. Women are there to show silent support." Look at that, the patriarchy isn't dead after all. "As a sign of respect, no boss can speak to another's wife or girlfriend." How suffocating. I can't imagine living a life of complete suppression. "You're permitted to speak with the other women if you choose. But I'd prefer you keep quiet, keep that sassy mouth of yours shut and just observe."

I have every intention of watching you and all the other bosses. "Of course, Katsuo."

"It's imperative that you understand whatever is discussed at the meeting can never be repeated or discussed with anyone other than me."

"I have no intention of telling anyone about your business." Not until after I kill you, then I might tell Ben.

"Good girl." He smacks my butt and chuckles. It sounds creepy coming from him, not sexy at all. Katsuo strolls ahead of me to the elevator, where his men and Tyler have all congregated. The door opens. Katsuo and I both enter, followed by his men and Tyler. Tyler positions himself in front of me and sneaks a look over his shoulder. Katsuo takes my hand and lifts it to his mouth, kissing my knuckles. "So beautiful." *So cringy.*

We head down to the garage, where the cars are already assembled and waiting. The middle black SUV has the back door open. Tyler is cautious as he looks around and walks ahead to the waiting SUV. He guides me into the vehicle, then Katsuo slides in. "Wow," I say as I look around to see where everyone is. Tyler slides into the front passenger seat.

"What?"

"There's so much tension. It's like you're all waiting for something to happen."

"These meetings can be tense, but we also have to be prepared."

"What for?" I ask with innocence.

"Police or a traitor."

"I understand the police part, but traitors?"

"It's happened in the past, so we're just overly careful. We wouldn't want to be caught out." The cars leave the underground garage and all travel in formation. Katsuo isn't in a talking mood, so I take this opportunity to use his silence for my own recon. I watch where we travel and take mental notes on everything. Katsuo rubs at the back of his neck several times and wipes his hands down the front of his pants. The biggest giveaway to his nervousness is how he tenses and relaxes his jaw. He's nervous, and I'm damned excited. Finally, I'll be a step closer to ending him and whatever bullshit he's got going on in Bankstown Creek.

The drive takes us through a rural area, where the houses are large and the grounds even bigger. The house we approach is best described as an old castle that's never fallen into disrepair. The property is completely isolated with nothing around it for miles. It's the perfect place to host heads of one of the deadliest organizations in the world. *Fun.*

The sheer number of limousines already there tells me there are a lot of bosses here. Hmm, this could pose an issue for me if I'm recognized. However I doubt it, considering I've only ever done one job for a Yakuza boss and that was in Japan. I'll assess the risk once inside. If it's going to be a problem, I'll find a solution. I always do.

Our car pulls up in front of the castle, where a butler opens the door. Katsuo slides out, then offers me his hand. "Thank you." He buttons his suit jacket and straightens his shoulders.

The gravel crunches beneath my shoes as we walk into the castle.

My skin pebbles with excitement and my stomach tightens and releases. My pulse speeds up as every single one of my senses comes to life with a vibrant buzz. "Don't be scared, Treasure," Katsuo whispers as he tightens his fingers around mine. I'm not scared, I'm damned excited. "Just remember the rules."

"I will."

He ushers us up a flight of grand, winding stairs, then toward a room at the back. There are a number of men standing outside the door and more lining the long, wide hallway. One of the men looks at me, then Katsuo before opening the door. We both step inside to find another door. This one is thick, like a bank vault. It has two large bolts that lock into place. The door opens and inside is a smoky room filled with men and women. I count eighteen men, who all turn as one to see who's coming into the meeting.

They all stand as Katsuo strides in with me following behind. "Sir," some greet as they bow. He leads me over to the head of the table where there's a space and flicks his gaze to the seat behind his.

The other women all look over toward me before speaking quietly among themselves.

Katsuo sits at the head of the table and all the other men sit after he does. Interesting. He's the boss. Hmmm. As they say, the bigger they are, the harder they fall.

I sit back and watch as the men all take their places at the table. There are two familiar faces I'm aware of. They don't know me, because they were targets that had the hit revoked on the eleventh hour. I know I can take them down, *easily*.

There's a man sitting at the table to Katsuo's right who's glaring at me. From where I sit, I can see Katsuo is clearly unimpressed with the man. He has a prominent scar running from the top of his left brow down to the bottom of his left cheek. His left eyelid is severely deformed and doesn't close fully when he blinks. He's borderline emaciated and his face is pale and sunken.

I listen as Katsuo initiates the conversation, welcoming everyone who's travelled from near and far. His voice booms, commanding the attention of nearly every set of eyes in the room, except for one—Scar Man. He continues to examine me closely. "What are you looking at?" Katsuo stops talking mid-sentence to address Scar Man.

"I know her," Scar Man says in a deep voice that sounds like a lifetime of damage from smoking three packs a day.

"What?" Katsuo halts the meeting and shifts back in his chair, turning for a second to give me a confused look. My own façade tightens.

"I know her," Scar Man repeats.

"How?" Katsuo questions.

"I can't recall, but I know she's been around our kind before." Almost like a tennis match, everyone's eyes shift to look at me. *Fuck.* I sit back in the seat trying to make myself small, like I have no idea what Scar Man is talking about.

Katsuo turns to stare and silently question me. My eyes widen as my shoulders slowly rise in a shrug. The air in the room is pulsating as a dark restlessness fills the space. Tension is climbing and if this isn't dealt with, there's going to be war. I'll take on every one of these motherfuckers, slaughter them and leave without a fucking mark on my body. My scalp prickles with unease. I'm making a mental note of who to go through first, who to use as a human shield, and who's the weakest.

"Impossible," Katsuo says. "I had her thoroughly investigated."

The silence in the room is palpable and edgy. This is how I feel seconds before I pull the trigger on my sniper rifle. This is delicious and exciting.

Scar Man stands and slams his hand in a weak attempt at gaining control. "I tell you, I know her." He points toward me. "Your investigation is flawed."

Damn, I won't have to do anything to him because Katsuo hates being shown up in front of people. He's going to take care of Scar Man for me. "You dare insult me?"

"I'm sorry, but..."

God, I wish I could have a tub of popcorn as I watch Scar Man being torn apart by Katsuo before my turn with Katsuo. In a fraction of a second, Katsuo is up and has Scar Man in an unnatural headlock. Scar Man's face instantly reddens from lack of oxygen and his eyes fill with tears while he gasps for air. I stare as all the air slowly leaves his body. "Does anyone else have any concerns about my property?"

Ew, property? I don't think so. Scar Man's body quickly stops fighting and becomes limp. No, I can't have Scar Man dead yet, I need him to know he was right before I take his life. Katsuo releases Scar Man and lays a boot into his side causing him to groan in response.

I stand from my designated space and calmly walk over to Scar Man. I carefully kneel and check for a pulse. I lean down and put my ear to his mouth before whispering, "You're right." Not a soul other than him heard me. To everyone watching, I look like a woman who has a caring nature. *I don't,* but that's how I look, and that's the most important thing here. Showing a softer side in a room full of ruthlessness and evil. If only they knew they had nothing on me.

I stand and look to Katsuo, offering him a small smile of acceptance. "I'm proud of you, Treasure." He gives me a kiss on the cheek as he leads me over like a damned queen sitting on her throne. "Now." Katsuo gives me a small wink before commanding everyone's attention. "Let's get back to the meeting." Katsuo returns to his seat and looks around the table. "First we need to talk about threats." He goes on to listen to everyone reporting about the Russians, Italians and local small timers creating problems for them.

"There's been movement on the East Coast. The James family has gone into hiding, but the Pace family is beginning to show themselves," one of the younger guys at the table says. He's dressed impeccably in a fitted suit. They do say, dress for the job you want, not the one you have.

Katsuo releases a loud belly laugh and shakes his head. What did I miss? "Knowing you, Daiki, you would've sent them a subtle warning."

The young man, Daiki, smirks cheekily. He reaches across and grabs his cigarette packet. He taps them on the table and takes one out, pops it between his lips, and lights it. "I might've sent them a message. I shut down all the money laundering we don't control." He sits back in his chair and slings his arm over the side. "Anyone who's not laundering for us is probably afraid."

"Excellent work," Katsuo congratulates him. "How much more do you have to do?"

"The James family looks like they've thrown in the towel, they've gone into hiding but I'll find them and take them out. However, the Pace family are a tight unit and their security at this stage is impenetrable."

"You can't get through?"

"Not yet. But I'm confident I'll get there soon."

Interesting. I know of the James family, and have heard of the Pace family but have never had anything to do with them. Neither family has hired me for any purpose. "What message have you sent out to the launderers?" Katsuo asks.

Yes, what message have you sent, Daiki? "I had them taken out," Daiki replies as the corner of his lips tug up into a sinister smirk. "I offered them the opportunity to join us, but they declined." He takes in a sharp drag of his cigarette. "I liked some of them too. But they preferred to stay loyal to their old boss rather than join us."

Katsuo sits straighter, as if he's proud of Daiki. "Good. Make an appointment to come see me this week." He turns his body toward where Scar Man is now sitting, rubbing his throat. "The trafficking?" he asks in a deadpan voice. If he's talking about human trafficking, I'm going to lose my shit.

"None of the cattle have given us problems, and demand has increased." Fuck. They're moving women and children? I find I'm consciously controlling myself. I keep my breath steady while I unroll my hands from the fists I've made.

"Takumi, I want to see you this week too. Make it sooner than later."

"Of course," Scar Man replies and flashes me a quick scowl.

"I've found a new lab that I've kept an eye on for a while now. I needed to wait for it to fall off the radar of the local police. The plant had high success before it was raided by police and federal agents. I'm going to need a team to run it."

"What are we running?"

"Crystal meth," Katsuo says.

"I've got a cook," one of the men says.

"Are you referring to Mr. Crane?" Katsuo asks. The man nods. I know who Mr. Crane is. But I had no idea he cooked for the Yakuza. "Good."

"I'll run it," Daiki offers. "Where is it?"

"Bankstown Creek," Katsuo replies. *Oh shit.* He's been scoping out the plantation Mancini was using before I killed them all.

There's a collective groan of understanding that comes from the table. "Mancini never repaid his debt to us," Scar Man says.

"No, and both he and his son never surfaced again. They were investigating someone and had asked for our help, but they weren't worth the risk of taking out the person they wanted help with."

"Who was the person?" Daiki asks. "Should I go ahead and set up a team to find him?"

"I never got a name on the person, only that they were a new threat who'd shown up."

"Feds? Police? Who?"

"No idea," Katsuo replies. I know who they're talking about... *me*.

Although I'm listening, a recalled memory flashes into my mind. Ethan was in the bathroom, about to die and he told me about the money his father owed. I blink several times as I swallow. This has come full circle; Mancini owed Katsuo and Katsuo is going to collect by starting up this operation in Mancini's Bankstown Creek factory.

Not on my watch.

"I'll start asking questions, see what I can find out," Daiki says.

I wet my lips and add Daiki to my list of the people I need to take out.

"Weapons?" Katsuo asks.

Now we're talking my love language. "We've got a shipment of ninety thousand units coming in via Pakistan," says an older man sitting across from Scar Man.

"Any problems?" Katsuo asks.

"It's been an easy shipment so far. However, now that we lost our inside man in Bankstown Creek, we've approached one of the other staff and are waiting for her response."

"Waiting for her response?" Katsuo asks with disdain. "We don't wait for responses. Get it done." Katsuo points aggressively toward the man.

Her? Who are they talking about? The new deputy? What's her name? Adele? I need to warn Ben that he has another rat in his ranks.

The rest of the meeting is all useless bullshit I'm not interested in. I need to figure out a way to slip past Tyler and get over to Bankstown Creek to warn Ben.

As the meeting ends, the table begins to clear with Katsuo taking time to talk to everyone individually. I must say, although I can't stand him, he's a good businessman who has his team under control.

Scar Man is one of the last left to leave, and when he glances at me, I give him a small wink. Yep, you've made my list. I might even push you toward the top of the list, or I'll let your own imagination screw with you.

Once everyone has left, Katsuo and I head out toward the car. "Thank you for bringing me, Katsuo," I say as Tyler and Katsuo's team lead us out of the house.

"Did you like the house?"

I don't give a rat's ass about something so frivolous. "I wish I saw more of it." No, I really don't. I just wish there was more said at the meeting.

As we wait for the car, he engulfs me in his arms and pulls me into his body. His erection is pressing into me. "I'll bring you back any time you want." Can I go vomit now? "What did you whisper to Takumi?"

"I told him not to underestimate you." Let's feed Katsuo's ego.

"You make me so proud." He kisses my neck as his hands slide down to my butt where he squeezes.

"Tell me about this beautiful house," I say, hoping I can drag his horny attention away from me.

"It's owned by the heads in Japan and it's used for meetings, or for the men to whisk their spouses or their girlfriends away for a dirty weekend." Tyler opens the back door of the SUV where I slide in before Katsuo does. "Should I bring you here for a dirty weekend?" He waggles his brows at me.

Only if his dirty weekend aligns with mine. Guns, knives, torture. *Fun.* "Sometime soon," I promise.

"I think..." he pauses and reaches into his pocket. Katsuo looks at his phone and furrows his brows. "Yeah," he answers the call. His chin lowers and his eyes close. "When?" He smacks his hand on the back of the passenger seat. "How many?" His jaw tightens as he shakes his head. "Find the fuckers who did this and kill them." Katsuo lowers his phone as he turns to look outside.

"What is it?"

"Don't talk to me," he warns in a small voice.

Really? You think I'm not going to push you? I scoot over closer to him and lay my hand on his thigh. "It'll be okay." I can hear him grinding his teeth. The muscle in his leg is tense with anger. "I'm sure it'll be fine," I push a little more. "Don't worry."

He turns and slaps me across the face. "I told you not to talk to me," he warns.

It's not the hitting I love. It's pushing him to the point of losing control, which is easy with him. Antagonizing someone is one of my favorite things to do, especially when I know it hits certain nerves. "Fine, you don't have to talk to me," I say with a pout and as much sadness as I can muster.

Instantly, he regrets hurting me again and drapes his arm over my shoulders to pull me closer to him. "I'm sorry, but you should be quiet when I asked you to." *Dick.* "It's just we lost a shipment."

"Of guns?" Please no, not the guns.

"Of girls."

My stomach roils with disgust. Fucking pig. I can't wait to tear him apart. "Girls? As in slaves or girls who'll be raped and tortured?" I have a newfound reason to despise him. Now, my façade must stay firmly in place and I have to work harder and faster to bring him and his operations down.

"Does it matter?" he says so matter-of-factly. "That shipment has lost me a lot of money, and whoever did this has to die," he says with no remorse for the girls he's stolen, held captive, and sold for his own profit.

You'll die by my hand, Katsuo. You have no idea what I'm capable of.

CHAPTER TEN

ANNA

I haven't slept a moment since we've been back at Katsuo's penthouse. He's beside me, sleeping like the dead. I could easily slit his throat and be done with him, but I know the moment he's gone, there are ten people waiting to take his place.

I can't stop thinking about the shipment of women who've been rescued from whatever fate he was sending them to. I turn to look at him and clench my jaw as I refrain from smothering him in his sleep.

The only way I can successfully tear this down is from the inside. To listen, learn and gather all the information I can so I know who the players are once I destroy Katsuo.

The light breaks in through the window, and I know I need to get out of bed or I'll end up killing him right now. I have to put distance between us because I can feel my rage twitching and edging toward the uncontrollable. And control is something I live by. I put on a robe and head out of the bedroom to find coffee. The chef is already in the kitchen.

He acknowledges me with a small smile and a nod. "Coffee, Miss Moore?"

"Please." I sit on one of the barstools and wait for him to bring me a coffee. I use these moments to control my breath, and in turn, control my fury toward Katsuo.

I need to harness the rage into hurting him when the time is right. Not a moment before. "Would you like some breakfast?" John, the chef, asks when he hands me the mug.

"That would be good, thank you."

"How does bacon and eggs sound?"

"Delicious," I reply and smile warmly toward him.

"Miss Moore," Tyler announces as he walks into the kitchen. "You're up early."

"I am." Because I've been thinking of ways to kill your boss. "So are you." I flash him a look from over my coffee mug.

"Always need to be prepared." He walks over to one of the cabinets and removes a mug before pouring himself some coffee. "Why are you up so early?" He leans against the cabinets and sips his hot beverage.

"Always need to be prepared," I say and smirk.

Tyler glances down at his coffee and lifts his chin only to straighten and place the mug on the counter. His reaction tells me Katsuo is walking into the kitchen.

His arms wrap around me and he kisses my temple. "Why aren't you in bed?"

"I couldn't sleep," I reply as I pick at my bacon. In this moment, I'm imagining every possible way I could kill him. Would Tyler attempt to stop me? Would John? "What are you doing today?"

"I have another meeting that I'm running late for." Katsuo looks over at Tyler. "Tyler," he acknowledges with a grunt.

"Mr. Vang." Tyler takes his coffee and makes a hasty exit out of the kitchen.

"Am I coming to this meeting with you? It won't take me long to get ready."

"No, stay here. Besides, Takumi should be arriving soon, but I'll be back before he does." Well, now this has the potential of being interesting. I was going to go home, but now I think I'll stick around and wait for Scar Man to arrive. "Do you want to go shopping?" He reaches for his wallet but I wave his hand away. "What?"

"I'm not going shopping. I have some work to do this afternoon, but I'll wait for you to return."

One of Katsuo's men appears in the kitchen. "Mr. Vang, your car is ready."

Katsuo gives him a curt nod and walks around to give me a kiss on top of the head. Everything about him makes my skin crawl and my blood boil. "I'll see you soon, Treasure."

Stupid fucking nickname. "Bye. Take care." I wouldn't want you hurt before I get a chance to do it.

I finish my breakfast and head back up to Katsuo's room so I can get ready for the day.

Damn it, Tyler is with Scar Man which means I can't get in to see him. But, it also means I have an opportunity to get out of here and make contact with Agent. I wander through the penthouse to find Tyler standing outside the library. "I'm ready to leave, Tyler," I say to him.

"Mr. Vang instructed me to stay here with..." He points toward the door.

"That's okay, I'll meet you at home."

"No, Miss Moore, please. I'd appreciate if you stay here."

"Sure thing." Let me get on that. I head toward the elevators and press the button down to the garage. Unfortunately, my car isn't here, and I know they'll be tracking the cars in the garage, so I'm going to have to make it quick when I return home because Katsuo or Tyler will be arriving hot on my tail. Thankfully, no one sees me leaving, but they'll know when I get to the garage. One of his men is waiting when I reach the garage.

"Miss Moore," he says when he sees me. He straightens and stomps out a cigarette.

"Take me home."

"Um." He searches over my shoulder for Tyler.

"For God's sake." I whip the phone Katsuo has given me out of my pocket and call him. He doesn't answer. "He's in a meeting. Do you really want to be the one who bothers him?" I hold out the phone to his man who looks down, confused. "Fine. Let's try calling him again, and you can explain it to him."

"It's okay." Good, my bluff worked. He whistles to one of the others and gestures to bring a car around. I'm not waiting long before the car pulls up and the guy waiting with me opens the rear door.

The drive home takes what feels like forever, and I'm on tenterhooks hoping Katsuo doesn't call the driver and have him return me. So, I send Katsuo a message. **One of the driver's is taking me home, I have work to do.**

His reply is instant. *Is Tyler with you?*

No, he's back at the apartment.

Turn the car around and wait for him.

You have a car parked right outside my house. Nothing will happen. I'm going home.

The phone vibrates and I know it's Katsuo. "You have to the count of three."

"I'm not a child. So, the answer is no."

"Your safety is my only concern."

I want to snicker at how ludicrous he is. The only person who needs to be kept safe is him, from me. "I have work to do, and there's always a car outside my house. I can't wait around for you all day, Katsuo."

He inhales deeply and I hear a click of his tongue. "You really know how to push me, don't you?"

"I've got a lot of work piled up, so I won't be able to see you tonight."

"I'll pick you up in the morning."

"Why?"

"Because I said so." He hangs up without allowing me a chance to respond.

He's such an ass, but at least I get some peace and quiet without having Tyler hanging around.

Once home, I'm met by another one of Katsuo's men at the door. "I'm to secure the premises before you enter," he says in a deadpan voice.

Joy. "Sure." He walks in ahead of me and checks every room before silently leaving.

I double-check everything before going to my laptop and opening it up. I head into the bathroom, and open up one of the secret compartments to remove a phone. I turn it on and call Agent. He answers the phone with, "I've been worried."

"For me or for them?"

"A bit of both. Mostly them though. We need a GPS signal on you at all times, at least until this job is over."

"There's no way that's possible. Not with him. He's paranoid to the max."

"We also have another problem. I've managed to squash developments, but this concerns you too."

"How so?"

"There's been chatter coming out of Washington. Specifically, the J. Edgar Hoover building."

"The FBI?" I ask. I've managed to stay under their radar since I started. They know of me, but don't know who I am. "What's the word?"

"There's been talk about a problem in Bankstown Creek."

"Bankstown Creek is a small town that wouldn't draw attention unless they know what they're looking for. What exactly do you know?"

"The assassination of the hardware couple, a few others, and a dirty cop." I tap on my chin as I try to think a way to navigate around this. "Want to hear what they're calling you?"

"They have a name for me?"

"You're known as the girl with the golden aim."

I scrunch my nose at the stupid name. "Are you kidding me?"

"Nope." Agent chuckles. "Not at all."

"If I was male I'd be known as the man with the golden aim. Sexism at its best."

"Hey, I didn't make up the name, someone over at the FBI did."

"Find them so I can kill them," I say half joking, half not.

"Alright," Agent replies.

"No, don't. I can't kill someone for christening me with a stupid name. Jesus, why don't they just refer to me as 15, like everyone else?"

"I don't make the rules," Agent adds. "How long before you're done with the target? You're leaving a lot of money on the table by staying there. I have three jobs lined up, all paying well above your asking price."

"Hmmm." I nod my head. "Time to put my fee up."

"Does that mean I can buy my boat?"

"It means, time for me to raise *my* fee up."

"You can't blame a guy for trying."

"I need you to look into a few people."

"Who?" I give Agent a list of people I need information on, then go on to describe what I want him to do in detail with his findings. Agent has his job cut out for him, but that's why I pay him the big bucks.

When I hang up, I go to my bedroom window and check outside. While keeping an eye outside, I dial Ben. "Yeah," he answers.

I smile hearing his voice. "I've missed you," I say.

"Anna." He releases a long breath. "Where have you been?"

"I'm in deep with something."

"What is it? What can I do?"

"Nothing, but there are a few things I've heard that you need to know about. You've got someone dirty at the station and you need to keep an eye out on everyone. Plus, my current target has indicated there's a policewoman they've approached for information. I don't know if they're the same people, but I think it might be Adele they're talking about."

"Adele? Who's been talking?"

"It doesn't matter who. Just be careful and keep vigilant, okay? I also think the assassinations will stop now too."

"What have you done?"

"Me? Nothing. But, I have information that indicates the assassinations will stop."

"How?"

I see the black car approaching. Shit, Tyler will be here in a few seconds. "I have to go."

"Let me help if you're in trouble. You don't have to do this alone."

"It's not anything I haven't done before. Be careful, and I'll be in touch again when I can." I hang up and turn the phone off, making it untraceable. Just as I hide the phone again, I hear the front door opening.

"Miss Moore," Tyler calls.

"Bathroom," I respond. I flush the toilet, wash my hands, and walk out into the bedroom where Tyler is standing by the door. "Didn't take you long."

"I'd prefer if you don't do that again."

"Prefer?" I challenge. "What you're saying is you're not completely opposed to me leaving without you."

Tyler runs his hand through his hair before scratching at his eyebrow. "Don't do that again."

"Yes, sir." I fake a salute.

"I have one job, and that's to protect you. Can you please not make it any harder than it already is?"

Huh. Interesting. Why would he say *harder than it already is?* What exactly does he mean by that? "Well." I step toward him, and he counters. "As much as this is a *lovely* chat, I have work to do," I say with sarcasm. "Do you mind closing the door?"

Tyler straightens, shakes his head, and exits my bedroom, leaving the door open. Smart-ass. At least I know I don't have to see Katsuo until tomorrow which gives me a night of peace.

It also allows me to do research. Although I'd rather be in bed with Ben doing dirty, *dirty* things.

Chapter Eleven

— ⬩ —

Anna

"Wake up, Treasure." Ugh. Why does he have to be here? I finally managed to fall asleep after four in the morning and this fucker is here trying to wake me. Inconsiderate ass. "Come on, you need to wake up now. Can't spend the entire day in bed." He shifts off the mattress. "Unless you want to spend it in bed with me."

Nothing in this world can force me to stay in bed with Katsuo all day. I'd rather suffocate him than have to have sex with him again. "I'm awake; stop bothering me." I flick my hand at him.

"You need to get up. We have things to do today."

Like killing you? *I wish.* "Yeah, yeah, I know." I push the covers off and without even looking at Katsuo I head into the bathroom. When I return, Katsuo has left the bed. *Thank God.* This gives me enough time to change and get ready for the day. "Where are we going?" I ask as I walk out to find Katsuo in my kitchen going through all the drawers. "What are you doing?"

"It occurred to me that I haven't inspected your house."

"What?" I ask as I shake my head. "After all the shit you've done, you still don't trust me? What the fuck, Katsuo?"

"In my business, I always need to be careful of outsiders."

I furrow my brows and lean against the wall as Katsuo continues to tear my kitchen apart. I lower my head as I stare at my shoes. "It's because of that Takumi guy, right? He's planted some bullshit story in your head about me."

"He has nothing to do with it."

"Fine, then put me on the lie detector again. Or better still, leave. Take your stupid men, and get the fuck out of my house. I don't need this shit from you, Katsuo." This is sure to antagonize him. What will happen is he'll lose his control, smack me, then apologize for hurting me.

I'm prepared.

I'm doing this because I need to push him so he thinks he has absolute control over me. He needs to have full trust and faith that he's the alpha, and I'm not even strong enough to be a beta. Thing is, I've never been an alpha, I'm an omega. The anti-hero who lives by her own rules and doesn't need to rise to the top because she's already there.

He slams the drawer he's been rifling through and straightens. "Watch your tone," he warns in an eerily calm voice.

"You watch yours," I reply matching his vibe. I pull my shoulders back and stare at him.

The moment is held hostage by silence and neither of us is backing down.

Now we're getting somewhere. Katsuo's nostrils flare and his eyes widen with rage. I've talked back to him, challenged him, and he hates it.

He leaps over the counter and grabs my shirt by the collar. He lifts an open hand over his head and slams it into my face. He lifts his hand a second time and repeats the process.

"Please," I whimper as I cower away from him.

He immediately relaxes and takes a step back. Katsuo runs his hands over his head and knits them together on the back of his neck.

This is what I wanted. For him to lose his shit, then instantly feel a moment of remorse. For a man like Katsuo, the remorse is only ever short-lived. For me, it fuels the desire to buckle in until the very end.

"Treasure," he starts as he steps forward.

"No!" I hold my hand up to him. "You don't get to treat me like this."

"I'm sorry. I'm so sorry." He falls to his knees in front of me and hugs my legs. A small smile stretches my face as I limply stay in his arms. I've got him where I want him. He sees me as property he can rule with fear. I see him with a bullet to the head. "Come on, let me take you out."

"I don't want to go anywhere."

He stands and pulls me into his arms. "I'm taking you shopping; you can buy anything you want." He tightens his embrace as he kisses my forehead. "Then we'll go back to the penthouse where I'll have someone give you a massage and a spa treatment and whatever else you want."

"I don't want to go anywhere with you if you don't trust me, Katsuo."

"I do, I'm just..." He intakes a sharp breath. "I'm sorry. I shouldn't have suspected you at all. I've been under so much stress, then yesterday with Takumi, and—"

"He scares me." Jeez, can I lay it on any thicker?

"I'll always protect you." Queue the vomit. "You never have to worry about anyone as long as you're with me."

I take several breaths before backing away from Katsuo. "I need the bathroom."

Katsuo slinks his arm around my waist and walks me to the bathroom. Once inside, I look in the mirror at the damage he's done to my face. The bruise that was fading is now replaced with a fresh red mark. The more he does, the slower and more painful his death will be. But I still don't have all the information I need yet. I need to get to Takumi and figure out what he knows and, more importantly, what he's told Katsuo before I can end this.

When I finish in the bathroom, I head out to where Katsuo is sitting on the edge of the bed, his phone to his ear. "I'll be there shortly," he says before ending the call. "Change of plans."

"You have to go."

"You're coming with me. Get your shit together." His entire body language has changed. He's clearly agitated, but not at me. *Interesting.*

"Where are we going?"

He abruptly stands and points his finger at me. "Don't fucking try me today, Anna."

I love getting under his skin. "I just asked where we're going."

Katsuo darts out the room and opens the front door. "Hurry up," he bellows.

I have no idea where we're going, and I wish I could take one of my guns in case I need it. But I still can't risk my identity being known until I have all the pieces of the puzzle and I'm ready to end him. I take nothing more than my phone and keys and jog to catch up to Katsuo, who's now in the car.

Tyler is waiting by the front door. He holds his hand out for my keys and when he sees the fresh red mark on my face, he lowers his chin and looks down at the ground. "Miss Moore," he mumbles. He flicks a quick glance at my face, mostly at the red mark. "Are you okay?" He locks the door slowly, waiting for my answer.

"I'll be fine."

Tyler's hesitant steps tell me he wants to say something, but by the time we get to the car he's remained quiet. "Miss Moore." He opens the back door and waits until I slide in. I get the distinct feeling Tyler doesn't like the way Katsuo treats me. Little does he know I have a plan, and that plan involves death—Katsuo's.

The car navigates away from my house and I keep my head facing forward, though sneak small glances over at Katsuo. His lips are pulled back in a scowl while his hands are balled tightly into fists. Something is happening and it's pushing him to the point of silent rage.

It doesn't take me long to figure out the car is heading toward the penthouse. The car pulls up to the underground garage, where it stops near the elevators. Katsuo exits the car before it comes to a full stop. Tyler is out and has the back door open for me.

"Katsuo," I call.

He stops walking and turns toward me. His jaw is clenched together and his eyes are wide with anger. "I'll speak to you in…"

The entire garage shakes with a low, deep rumble that vibrates all around us.

I know that sound. The walls of the garage shudder and debris falls from them. I look to Tyler who's frozen on the spot.

"Bomb!" I hear someone scream in panic.

My heart leaps into my throat as my pulse quickens with an excited buzz. "Get her out of here," I hear Katsuo yelling.

Fuck no; I want to be in the middle of it. I want to tear Katsuo's throat out and leave him here under the guise of the explosion. This may very well be the opportunity I need. "Anna," Tyler screams as he throws his body over mine protectively.

"Get her to the castle."

No! No, I need to stay here and take Katsuo out.

Tyler pushes himself over me while cloaking my body with his. "I need to get you to safety," he says as he pushes me toward the garage door.

"Stop! I need to get back there." I try to tear away from him, but the only way I can break free is if I hurt him. And I'm not prepared to blow my cover quite yet, because this is bigger than just Katsuo.

Tyler's sheer weight propels me under the garage door that's still half open from when we arrived. He quickly grabs me by the upper arm and pulls me away from the building that's shattering. Outside, there are people fleeing as the building shakes with yet a third explosion.

People are trying to get away in fear of what may happen. I look up toward the penthouse to see most of it completely dissolved. What the fuck has happened? Who did this? Whoever caused that explosion was clearly after Katsuo.

Tyler grabs me around the waist and throws me effortlessly into an SUV. I hate having to conceal my identity, but at the moment, it's the only way forward.

"Drive," he yells at the driver.

"We have to help," I say as I try the door handles only to find they've been locked. "There are people back there who need our help." The driver speeds away, ignoring my loud protests. "Stop!" At this stage, I truly don't care if Katsuo lives or dies, but the innocent people who are all collateral damage shouldn't have to pay with their lives because of him.

"Keep going," Tyler counters my plea.

I look at the doors and know there's no way I'll be able to break the glass. I'm in one of the safest vehicles there is. Bulletproof glass, flame-resistant metals and run-flat tires. Nearly nothing can get in, and even less can get out.

I hit my hand on the back of the passenger seat out of frustration. "We can't go back," Tyler says.

"Whatever," my voice is filled with tension. No one is speaking as the air pulses with pressure. Tyler receives a call, but he doesn't speak. He simply nods, then hangs up. "What happened?"

"There was a bomb."

"Obviously, Tyler, or the place wouldn't have exploded."

"Mr. Vang is investigating." Of course, he is. "We're going to the castle." He glances at me over his shoulder, than returns his full attention to our surroundings. We're not being followed, no one is behind us. I've already sussed it out.

The remainder of the drive to the castle is shrouded in quiet. The driver makes no effort to slow down until we reach the estate. He pulls into the long driveway and stops the car outside the front doors.

"Wait in the car," Tyler instructs before exiting to walk toward the door of the castle, where he's met by another man. They engage in a brief conversation and Tyler nods his head several times. Tyler returns to the car and opens the back door for me. "Miss Moore." He steps to the side, waiting for me to slide out. "I'll show you up to your room."

"Who's here?" I ask as I do a silent inventory of everyone I see while we walk upstairs and down the wide corridor.

"There's only a handful of staff here. The butler, two housekeepers, a chef and a grounds person." He stops by a door and opens it.

"I see." The room is opulent, with a massive bed in the center and pricey artwork hanging on nearly every wall.

"You'll be safe here, Miss Moore."

I nearly laugh in his face but contain myself. "Thank you, Tyler."

"Is there anything else you might need?" Tyler stands at the door, waiting upon my answer.

"I do want to ask you something." He lifts his brows silently asking me for my question. "You seem to throw yourself on me every time you believe there's danger nearby."

He stands impassively blinking at me. "Your question?"

"Why do you do that?" I watch Tyler closely.

There's a small twitch beneath his left eye and he shoves his hands into his suit pants pockets. Tyler is reluctant to tell me something. "It's my job, Miss Moore. I'm paid to protect you."

He's clearly lying, so I turn the heat up a notch. "It's your job?" My brows rise and I smirk.

"Of course," this response comes naturally and easily.

"Okay then." Yep, he's certainly hiding something. I turn and walk over toward the double doors that open and lead out to a balcony.

"Stay away from the meeting room, and the basement."

"Of course," I reply as easily as Tyler did. Stay away from the basement he said. Next stop, the basement. Let's see what treats there are down there. "Thank you," I call as I now ignore him. I need Tyler out, so I can give myself some time before I head to the basement.

Finding the door that leads to the basement was hard enough, avoiding Tyler was even harder. The basement is creepy, like one of those horror movies, made even creepier by the various tunnels.

I turn the handle of the first door I come across and peek inside. Nothing out of the ordinary, it actually appears to be a storage room. I double-check the proximity of the next room, and the first one seems proportional. I close the door and check the next few rooms. All look normal, nothing to be alarmed about.

I turn the handle of the fifth room, and my stomach clenches. I step inside and look around. There's a massive mirror on the wall and a table with three chairs. But the thing that gives me a sick feeling in my gut is the various splotches of dried blood. The stench turns my stomach. I know what this room is; it's an interrogation room.

"You found my second favorite room of the house."

My skin breaks out into goose bumps when I hear the all too familiar voice. I turn to come face-to-face with someone I was planning to kill, only not yet. "Mr. Takumi," I say as I cast a wary eye down his body.

"Miss Moore, right?" he asks as he steps toward me, essentially forcing me further into the room. I straighten and try to move past him without replying. He grabs me, digs his fingers around my upper arm, and yanks me back toward him. "I can see why Katsuo keeps you around, I'm sure he won't mind me having a taste." He sucks my lobe into his mouth and presses his erection into my hip.

I shove at him but his hand has a firm grip on my upper arm. "You're such a good foot soldier, I wouldn't want Katsuo to kill you," I provoke with a sneer.

"I can do whatever I want with you, because no one can hear you down here." He waggles his brows and licks his lips. "Now sit down, you fucking whore." He pushes me toward one of the chairs.

Fuck, I might have to kill him here, but if I do it means I'll have to reveal myself. This might be the opportunity I need. I regain my posture and walk over to the chair. You want to play, so let's play. I sit back and show complete indifference to Takumi. If Katsuo is watching because this is a setup, I'll be careful with my words and body language.

But if it's not a setup, this fucker better be prepared for what I'll unleash.

"You go by Miss Moore, do you?"

I arch a brow. "It's my name."

"Your mouth might be smart, but you certainly aren't." I stare at him with complete disregard. "You're in a relationship with Ben Pearson."

What the actual fuck? My stomach churns as my heart rate jumps. "Who?" I ask as I tilt my head to the side. How the fuck does he know?

His one good eye squints at me as his thin lips pull up into a smile. His teeth are rotting out of his mouth. "You know who he is."

"Who *who* is?" I don't break my stare or posture. On the outside, I'm calm as fuck, on the inside, my mind is speedily attempting to figure out how he found out about Ben when Katsuo never has.

"If you don't know him, then it doesn't matter," he pushes as he waits for a reaction.

I shrug. "You're right, it doesn't." I push up and go to leave the room.

"Who the fuck told you to leave?" He leaps to his feet and grabs my arm again. "Now sit down before I fuck you into submission, you dirty fucking cunt." He shoves me back toward the chair.

Well look at that, Scar Man has anger issues. I sit and look up at him. "You're here for me, aren't you?" The look of satisfaction on his face confirms my question. "How did you know I was going to be here?"

"Katsuo told your idiot bodyguard to bring you here if there was ever an attack or if you took off like you did yesterday."

I stare at him when the puzzle pieces come together. "And you were the one to bomb the penthouse. Did you want me dead, or forced here?"

"I want you both dead, but I'll get to that."

"You want us dead? Why?"

"Because you're not who you say you are and Katsuo..." he pauses and chuckles lightly. "I deserve his position."

"You want the power."

"I want the money, and the power. Once you kill yourself, I'll then kill Katsuo."

Not only does Scar Man have anger issues, he's also delusional. *Nice.* "Huh," I huff as I nod with downturned lip. "So, I'm going to kill myself, am I?"

"Katsuo will arrive shortly, and when he does, I'll shoot him. Then you'll fall to your death and everyone will think you killed him then killed yourself."

I snort with laughter. "Sounds like a subpar mystery novel to me." Standing, I round the table and lean down to him. "I'll fucking gut you and feed you your own spleen," I whisper.

In a swift motion, he stands, grabs me around the neck, and slams me down on the table. I use my elbow to hit him in the chest, giving me only a few seconds to get to my feet. He lunges at me and punches me in the face before landing a kick to my stomach. This winds me and forces me to stumble back. Scar Man comes at me again, both his hands tightened into fists, ready to knock me out.

I lift my arms to protect my head, but this gives Scar Man the opportunity to punch my stomach again. I retreat, attempting to get past him to the door. But he grabs a fistful of my hair and slams my head into the wall. *Fuck, that hurt.*

My balance is thrown off, and I fall to the ground. He walks around to my side, ready to kick me in the ribs. I turn and punch into his knee, forcing him to the ground. It gives me only a few seconds' grace before he's up again and lays his foot straight into my side. "You fucking whore!" he yells.

A loud groan escapes as the pain reminds me to fucking kill him. I push up on my elbows but he manages to get me again. *Fucker.* He tries for a third time, but I catch his foot and turn it sharply. I hear a crack and know I've at the very least badly sprained his ankle if not broken it.

The pain radiating from my head and the blood dripping out of the wound on my forehead encourages me to take my time. "You're the fucking whore," I say as I manage to stand and kick him in the hip. I know I've broken that from the loud snap. His cries and falls to the floor, screaming to confirm it.

I'm ready to end him, snap his neck and fucking take his miserable life. But he pulls a fucking gun and aims. Bullets whoosh by from behind me. I turn and see Katsuo standing at the door with his gun pointed to Scar Man.

Blood oozes out of Scar Man's head. His eyes are wide and open. My only regret is he didn't die from my hand.

"What the fuck?" Katsuo turns to Tyler and hands him the gun. "Get her upstairs."

I stumble back, finally able to catch my breath. Tyler links his arm under my elbow to take some of my weight. "Use me as support."

"I'm okay," I manage to groan painfully.

"You sound and look like shit."

My breath is heaving as I try to regulate it. I've been in worse positions in the past, only Doctor was on hand to help me then. "It's just a little scratch."

"You're bleeding from a gaping wound on your forehead, and you're clutching your side while we walk. That doesn't look like 'just a little scratch.'" He takes in a sharp breath as we slowly navigate the steps. "What happened in there?" he asks as I probe my forehead with my free hand.

I think the glue has split open and the same wound from Prada has re-opened.

"Tyler, leave," Katsuo instructs as he takes the steps two at a time to get to us. Tyler reluctantly releases me for Katsuo to step in and take over. "What the hell happened down there?"

Think quick, Anna. "I was hungry and went searching for the kitchen. I took a wrong turn, and before I knew it, I was confronted by Takumi." I groan as we make our way up the stairs toward the bedroom.

"Did he just attack you? Because from where I was standing, it looked like you had the upper hand."

"I did," I admit. "By some freak of nature I was able to turn it around on him. I'm damn lucky, I'll tell you that," I say in an attempt to convince Katsuo.

"You're lucky I was there to kill him."

My big strong man. Seriously? I internally groan and roll my eyes. "I'm so glad you got there when you did. Only seconds before you shot him..." I make sure my voice trembles with fear. "...my life flashed before my eyes. All I could think was how I might not see you again." Okay, that one at the very least deserves an academy nomination.

"Doctor Hall will be here soon." He opens the door to the bedroom and helps me over toward the bed. "I'll always protect you, my love." I think my breakfast is making an attempt to escape. He lays me on the bed and runs his hand over my hair. "Stay here until Doctor Hall arrives. Tyler will be right outside the door if you need anything. I've still got some work to do." He steps toward the door.

"Takumi planted the bombs, he told me."

Katsuo stops and turns to look at me. His brows furrow and his lips purse together. "Takumi bombed the penthouse?" I sit up in bed and nod. "Why would he do that?"

"He wanted you dead. Actually, he wanted both of us dead," I correct.

"He was trying to convince me that you weren't you, and that you're in a relationship with some cop somewhere. He told me the name, but..." Katsuo shakes his head. "He wouldn't believe me." He pinches the bridge of his nose. "I even showed him the results of the polygraph." I arch a brow as I look away. "And he still refused to believe that you are who you say you are."

Smart man. But, he had to die. "I don't know what to tell you." Come on tears, just a couple is all I need. "He kicked me in the ribs, and he slammed my head onto the table. He called me a whore and a..." I shake my head. "I don't want to say it."

"What did he say?"

I lower my head and let my hair fall over my face like a veil. "He called me a cunt." I mean it's not the worst thing I've been called.

Katsuo returns to the bed and curtains me in a hug. *Ugh, get off me.* I relax my body into his and remain quiet, hoping this is enough for him to feel comfortable leaving. "I'm sorry he said that to you, but I've taken care of him now. He won't bother you again." Katsuo stands and heads toward the door. "Just rest until the doctor gets here." Without another word, he exits the room, leaving me on my own.

I take several deep breaths, pushing past what I suspect is a cracked rib. Closing my eyes, I center myself as I remember this is all for a cause. To protect Ben and Bankstown Creek.

The door opens suddenly and I open my eyes, ready for whatever is coming at me. Tyler walks in and crinkles his brows when he notices me startle. "Are you okay?" Behind him, Doctor Hall approaches.

"I'm fine," I say and look to the doctor. "I really don't think you need to be here."

"I'm glad you're a doctor now, Anna," she replies curtly. I like her spunk. She turns to Tyler and looks at the door. "Close that on the way out."

"Yes, ma'am," he replies and leaves the room.

She opens her doctor bag and comes to examine me. "I thought you would've gotten out of this lifestyle since the last time I saw you. You seemed like a bright girl."

Little does she know, I may have been forced into this life, but I'm making the absolute best I can of it. "Afraid not," I reply.

She dons gloves and looks at my head. "This will need stitches now. Two, maybe three." She returns to her medicine bag. "Shit," she grumbles.

"What is it?"

"I thought I had anesthetic to numb the area, I must've forgot to pack it."

"It only needs three stitches?" Doctor Hall nods. "I'll be fine without the anesthetic. Stitch me up." I lie back against the bed and close my eyes.

"Not without anesthetic. It will be too painful."

"Stitch me up," I say more firmly.

She silently cleans the wound, then starts stitching. "I have to say, you're a lot tougher than you look."

There's a reason for that. "Am I?"

"Maybe tougher than most of the men I've dealt with."

"I'm a woman, Doc, we're all tougher than men." I open my eyes to watch her concentrating on the stitches. "Every woman alive is a fucking warrior."

Doctor Hall smirks and nods. "Ain't that the truth." She finishes the stitches and cleans the wound. "You keep holding onto your side. Let me see if you have any cracked ribs."

"Oh, I do," I announce with confidence.

"What are my chances of getting you to the hospital?"

"On a scale of one to ten, one being unlikely and ten being accommodating. I'd say a solid minus fifty."

"So, there's still a small chance?" Doctor Hall snickers. She presses on my side as she examines me. "Without an x-ray I can't be sure, but it looks like you've got a cracked rib, or two."

"Thought so." She finishes her examination on me and I lower my t-shirt. "Thanks for your help, Doc."

She stands and stares at me for a few seconds before walking back to her medicine bag. "Take one of these, three times a day for the next five days." She hands me a small container with pills. "Antibiotics, because you don't want that to get infected." She gestures toward my forehead. I take the tablets from her and place them beside me on the bed. "In an ideal world I'd be speaking to you about the dangers of..." Doctor Hall pauses and looks around the bedroom. "...not going to the hospital," she finishes. But we both know what she's trying to say. She thinks I'm in danger and if I don't get out now, then I'll end up dead.

"Thank you," I say once again, essentially cutting her discussion short.

She balls her gloves together before shoving them into her medicine bag and closing it. "You know the deal. If you begin getting headaches, nausea or excessive tiredness make sure Mr. Vang takes you to the hospital," she says with a tinge of disappointment. Doctor Hall takes a breath and lowers her gaze before slightly nodding and turning to walk out.

She suspects I'll end up a gruesome statistic. She couldn't be any more wrong.

I turn over on the bed and start to think about Ben and how much I miss him. I wish I could see him, or even talk to him. But now, Scar Man has shown Katsuo how anyone can get to me. Katsuo's paranoia is going to peak and he won't let me out of his sight. Which means, seeing Ben will be even more difficult for me.

The door creaks open and I turn to see who's walking in. "Miss Moore, I'm checking to see if you're okay."

"I'm fine, Tyler." My acknowledgement should've sent him out of the room, but he hovers for a few seconds. "What is it?"

He stands taller and pulls his shoulders back. "Ma'am, I know I shouldn't say this," he pauses and looks out in the hallway before returning his attention to me. "I don't want you caught up in his business." I cock a brow and sit up in bed. "You should leave while you still can."

Why is Tyler hell-bent on protecting me? "What's going on? What aren't you telling me?"

He takes a small step toward me. "Please, I'm begging you, leave before it's too late." He pulls in a sharp breath and shoves his hands in his pockets. "You shouldn't be here when…"

"When what?" What's he planning? I need to check in with Agent to see what he's found out about Tyler, but I suspect this is going to become a challenge.

Tyler takes his hand out of his pocket and runs it through his hair. "This isn't a game, Miss Moore. Your life is in danger, but you can get out now and disappear. I can help you with that."

If I could get in contact with Agent, I'd have a better understanding of who Tyler is and what he's planning. I stand and walk over to Tyler. He counters with a small step backward. I lean into him and whisper, "This is exactly where I should be."

Tyler releases a groan and shakes his head in disappointment. "Yes, ma'am," he concedes, then leaves without saying another word.

Tyler doesn't give me vibes that he's evil, so who the fuck is he?

I'd better find out soon.

CHAPTER TWELVE

BEN

Fucking Yakuza.

Piece of shit fucking assholes.

The bane of my damn existence.

Fuck.

CHAPTER THIRTEEN

ANNA

I've been locked up in the castle for the last three days, healing. Katsuo has been absent, but his absence has given me time. Time to plot what I'm going to do, right down to the hammer I'll be using to hobble him. I'll take my time with Katsuo, draw as much pain as I can from him. And when he looks like he's about to die, I'll fucking keep him alive so I can torture him some more. His cries will spur me on to keep hurting him.

But instead, I have Tyler, who's now my permanent babysitter, attached to me.

Knock, knock.

"Yeah," I call as I flick through the TV channels. I hate sitting around and doing nothing. It's not in my nature to wait. I'm a take-charge kinda woman, not a sit around and wait for things to happen kinda woman.

Tyler enters and stands beside the sofa. I look to him, waiting for him to speak. "I've been thinking."

"Is that what that god-awful noise is?" He doesn't even crack a smile. "What?" I return my attention to the TV.

"You need to get out."

I'm sick of this argument with him. His need to save me is becoming intolerable. "Where's Katsuo?"

"He'll be returning in the next hour."

"That's not what I asked, Tyler." He clears his throat and lifts his chin. "Why are you so desperate to save me?"

"Because a woman like you shouldn't be here."

"Are you saying there are women who should be?"

"No, that's not what I'm saying. No one should be here, especially women." Out of the corner of my eye I notice his shoulders droop slightly. "This place..." He shakes his head. "It's like cancer."

"I know what goes on here."

"How can you be with a man like that who traffics girls and women?"

I turn the TV off and turn to face Tyler. "You're quite preachy for someone who makes his wage by protecting the man who traffics them."

"That's different."

"How so?"

Tyler's tongue peeps out to wet his lips. "Look," he starts. "You should leave while you can."

"Did you come in to lecture me? Because if you did, then..." I flick my hand at him dismissively.

A low grumble issues from his chest, but he finally leaves. Being stuck here in the castle, unable to communicate with Agent is infuriating. I need to get to a phone so I can call him, but it's too risky with Tyler watching me, and undoubtedly, Katsuo probably is too. I lift the remote and begin flicking through the channels on the TV again, attempting to quiet my mind.

But I'm getting antsy and I need to find a way out of here.

The door opens again, and I roll my eyes as I turn, expecting to see Tyler *again*. "Treasure. I've missed you, my love." Queue inner eruption of lava vomit.

I push the hatred I'm harboring aside and rise to my feet. "I've missed you so much," I say as I throw myself into his arms. His erection is pressing into me, and I scream internally because I know I'm going to have to put out. He does nothing for me. *He's no Ben.* "Where have you been? I thought you just dumped me here."

"I've had to procure another shipment."

I'll fucking stab your penis with a blunt pencil. "Did you get what you wanted?"

Katsuo digs his fingers into my hips as he steps toward the sofa and drags me to sit on his lap. "I don't want to talk about work, all I want to do is fuck you." He's calling trafficking women *work.* "I need you," he whispers as he kisses my neck.

Yeah, I need you like a hole in the fucking head.

BANG.

BANG.

BANG.

Tyler bursts through the door and yanks me off Katsuo's lap. He throws me to the floor and covers my body with his.

Oh, now we're getting somewhere. Something exciting is happening.

I turn to see Katsuo's men pull him up off the sofa and surround him protectively.

I struggle against Tyler. I need my guns, or just a weapon. Whatever is coming for us needs all of us to be protected. "Stay down," Tyler whispers in my ear. "Whatever you do, don't say a word."

"FBI, everybody down" is all I hear.

"Just do what they say," Tyler says in a low voice.

"Katsuo Vang, you're under arrest," one of the agents says. He reads Katsuo his Miranda rights before turning his attention to Tyler and me. The FBI pull Tyler off of me, handcuff him and lead him out of the room. "Miss Moore," the same agent says to me. They're not aware of who I really am, or they'd be addressing me as Anna Brookes.

There's a swarm of officers in the room. They're placing everyone in handcuffs and leading them away. "Yes," I respond.

"Turn around please." He dangles a set of handcuffs toward me.

"Why am I being arrested?"

"Human trafficking." Nothing angers me more than women and children being used in the trafficking industry. I grind my teeth together and don't speak. A female agent leads me out of the room and down the staircase to vehicles lined up in the drive. Everyone else from the house is being herded into the back of the vans.

I don't see Katsuo or Tyler, so I know they've already been taken. There's a helicopter flying overhead along with local police from Bankstown Creek and neighboring towns and the FBI. There are police dogs waiting on leashes with their handlers in case anyone attempts to make a run from the police.

I search for Ben, but he's not here. Not that I can see.

I know the FBI have nothing on me, and whatever charges they have will inevitably be dropped. Just like the staff of the house. I'm pushed into one of the cars which starts its journey toward town.

Shit, are we going to Bankstown Creek? Will I see Ben? Does Ben know what's happening? Of course, he would. *Shit.*

My stomach churns as we approach Bankstown Creek, but thankfully, we pass it. There's no way the small police station would be able to accommodate all of us. Besides, they'd need to take Katsuo somewhere off the grid so his men can't try and break him out. Somewhere safe, though unknown to the general public.

Suddenly, I know where they're taking us. There's a small ex-military compound about twenty miles out of Bankstown Creek. It was a training camp that was one of the best in its heyday, but hasn't been used in over ten years now. It has tunnels of underground bunkers and full of war simulation pods.

It's bulletproof, and off the grid.

And I know about it because Dad told me about it and promised he'd take me. He never got the chance, though.

There's no way any of Katsuo's men would know about this place. Katsuo is cocky and never even would've thought to have searched for this place. But I know about it.

The car rolls up to a security fence and it slowly opens.

This place is heavily, though discreetly, guarded. There are snipers on top of the buildings. Although they can't be easily seen, I know exactly what I'm looking for. A small reflection from the scope, a slight bump in the normally straight lines of the building.

This has been a while in the planning. They've done a thorough investigation of Katsuo and his business. They know exactly what they're getting themselves into, and they're fully prepared for anything they think may come at them.

If only they knew, the person they need to be afraid of is me. Katsuo is dangerous in a reckless way. I have the patience of a saint and can lay idle for a very long time before I strike.

"Let's go," the female agent instructs as she opens the back door and waits for me to shuffle out of the car.

I'm taken into the main building where there's a flock of officers, from FBI to local police milling around. I'm careful not to make it obvious that I'm looking for Ben.

"Take her to interrogation room three," one of the agents orders.

"Yes, sir." She grips onto my upper arm and guides me toward where she's been told to take me.

A man comes out of one of the rooms and looks at me. Jesus, what's happened to Ben? His hair is flat, his eyes are lifeless, and he looks like he hasn't slept in a week. My heart sparks to life when I see him because right now, nothing else matters. I was worried Scar Man had hurt him, but Ben is okay. He looks like shit, but he's alive.

"I'll take her," Ben tells the agent and leads me to the room.

"Oh, um." She looks around momentarily surprised. "Yes, sir," she replies and hands me over to Ben.

Ben drags me into the room he came out of. He closes the door behind me and immediately hugs and kisses me. "I can't take the cuffs off in case someone comes in. Don't talk to them at all," he whispers.

"What's happened to you? You look like shit."

"Listen to what I'm about to tell you, I don't know how much time we have. Sit, just in case." I sit in the chair and watch as he rounds the desk. "Don't talk to any of them, they don't want you and have nothing on you. They want Katsuo and everything about his operation. They intend to let you go."

I snort and shake my head. "He'll be taken care of." I watch him as he drags his fingers through his hair. "Why do you look like shit? What's happening?" I know something is going on with him.

"I need your help." My entire body sparks to life. Ben needs my help, and I'll do anything in my power to help him.

"What do you need my help with?" My heart pumps hard at the thrill of knowing I'm needed.

"Claire's gone." Two words have so many meanings. Gone where? Has she left her husband? Gone on an extended vacation? "She's been taken," he says in a voice no louder than a whisper.

"She's been kidnapped?"

Ben nods once as tears fill his eyes. "I need you to find her." He clears his throat and looks to his phone. "I got proof of life yesterday." He lifts his phone to show me a picture of Claire, blindfolded and tied to a chair with yesterday's newspaper on her lap.

I've got this. I'll find her, and kill whoever took her. I close my eyes for a moment and take a breath. I'm no longer Anna Brookes, I'm now 15. "First, you speak to no one, including Emily. You don't say a word until I'm released." He nods and visibly swallows. Ben is too close to this to see clearly. "You're going to have to trust me, Ben."

"I know, and I do."

"Second, be waiting for me the moment I'm released. Leave your service weapon at work, and have enough cash to last us until we can find her. No credit cards at all."

He nods again and looks up to me. This is why he's a mess, his sister has been taken and he's not coping.

The door opens and Ben instantly straightens. His own façade is now firmly in place, but I can see the fissures beneath the hardness. "We're ready for Miss Moore," a younger officer says.

"I'll bring her out," Ben replies.

The young officer steps to the side as he waits for me. Ben stands and pulls me up by my upper arm. I give him a small nod and smile. "I've got this," I whisper.

Ben leads me out, his hand now gently wrapped around my arm. He releases his grip and gently skims his hand down my arm. The touch is a well-kept secret between us. I feel the corner of my lips turn up in a slight smile. As the younger office grips my other arm to take me to interrogation, I see Katsuo walking toward me flanked by two officers.

His eyes narrow and his face reddens.

He saw Ben's touch. He knows. *Fuck.* Katsuo jerks back when he approaches Ben and stares at him. Ben stands to his full height, not backing down from the gauntlet Katsuo has silently thrown down.

In an environment where police are everywhere, Katsuo has no way of winning this, and he knows it. He bows his head in defeat, but not before giving me the side-eye and sneering heinously.

I feel the serpent sting travel through my body. I don't need his touch to know Katsuo intends to kill Ben and me.

There's no turning back now. When I get out, it'll be game on. But first, I need to help Ben find Claire. Then, I'll happily tear Katsuo apart.

The room is bleak and sterile. There's a camera in each corner and a massive two-way mirror. The chairs are uncomfortable and the room is silent. It's not designed for comfort. It's designed to make the person being interrogated feel like the walls are closing in on them.

A *regular* person would feel like that. Not me though. I'm indifferent. The FBI agent who busted into the bedroom at the castle walks into the room. He's an older man, perhaps in his mid to late fifties. His hair is an even mix of salt and pepper. His eyes are tired and suspicious; it must come with the job.

"Miss Moore," he starts as he sits and places a folder on the table.

"Could you take the cuffs off? It's not like I can go anywhere."

The agent flicks a quick glance over to a uniformed police officer, then gestures for him to remove the cuffs. "Miss Moore, my name is Special Agent Peter Trell. You may refer to me as Agent Trell."

The officer removes the cuffs, and I massage my wrists where they bit into my skin. "Am I under arrest?" The fact they don't know my real name tells me that I'm not.

"You're being held under the suspicion of aiding and abetting in human trafficking." Agent Trell straightens and pulls his shoulders back. For someone who has nothing on me, he's fairly confident he'll be able to get me to talk.

He has no idea I'm Anna Brookes, also known as 15. I have no intentions of giving anything up on Katsuo, because he and I have a special date once I find Claire and get her to safety.

"Aiding and abetting in human trafficking." I click my tongue and shake my head. "Doesn't sound too good, does it?"

"No, Anna it—"

"Miss Moore," I interrupt.

His eyes shift from the folder to me. "Pardon?" His brows shoot up while his lips flatten into a thin line. It amuses me to see how he's irritated with me.

"I expect the same courtesy I extend to you."

He swallows visibly as his lip curls in disgust. "As I was saying, *Anna*, no that doesn't sound good."

Annoying the FBI is so much fun. I take a moment to let the tension build in the room before arching a brow. "I'm sorry, Peter, I missed it. Am I under arrest or am I simply being held? There's a difference, and so far, no one has informed me that I'm under arrest or read me my rights. Huh, I wonder where my phone call to my lawyer is."

He completely ignores my question. "My superiors are only interested in Katsuo Vang and his operation. If you can help them, then we'll see what we can do for you."

Wow, vaguest sentence in the universe. "In exchange for seeing what you can do for me, what exactly do you want *from* me?"

"If you can provide us with information on Katsuo Vang's operations, take a look at mug shots and give us the descriptions of the people you've seen him with. If you could help us, then I'm sure we could take jail time off the table and offer you probation, maybe with community service." He sits back in the seat and crosses his arms in front of his chest. He thinks he has me at checkmate because he's used words that would normally have people quaking with fear.

I mirror his pose while concentrating on my facial features, schooling them to read like I'm considering his offer. "Wow, what an offer," I say while intently watching him. His lips relax as he thinks he has me. "But first, show me the evidence you have on me for my role in human trafficking."

The small smirk he was harboring instantly fades. "We don't have to show you anything. You're the one being held here."

"So, I'm being held, not arrested." I slink an arm over the back of my chair. "Evidence that I'm involved, then I'll talk."

Agent Trell licks his lips as he stares at the file that he hasn't opened once. I can bet there's not a God damned thing in that file about me. "You're playing a dangerous game for the wrong team, Miss Moore."

"The only team I'm on is my own."

He abruptly stands, snatches the file off the table, and walks toward the door. "I need to confer with my superiors."

"Do so. See what they say. No evidence, no information." I simply shrug.

He walks out with the other police officer who was in the room. This is where the waiting begins. They'll leave me in here for a few hours so I can mull over what they've said in hopes that I break and confess to whatever they want.

The moments turn into an hour. Then another, then another. They know, as do I, they have nothing on me. Not a shred of evidence. Nothing.

The hours keep stacking, and I patiently wait for someone to return.

The door finally opens and the female officer enters. "You're free to go, Miss Moore."

Wordlessly, I stand and walk out of the interrogation room with my head held high. I look for Katsuo, but he's nowhere to be seen. He'll be deep underground in one of the bunkers. But for now, I need to find Claire and worry about Katsuo later.

Agent Trell approaches and stops in front of me. "You may think what you're doing is protecting the man you love, but he's a monster and he deserves to go to prison for the rest of his life." I can't help but let my arrogance show by smirking as he speaks. "Do you think this is funny? Don't you have a conscience?"

"Is that all?" I reply, staring at him with a sneer.

He shakes his head and looks behind me. "Police Chief Pearson will return you to Bankstown Creek. If I were you though, I wouldn't go too far."

I can easily disappear and they'll never find me again.

But, for now, I have other priorities.

CHAPTER FOURTEEN

— • —

ANNA

Ben grabs me by the upper arm and pushes me along. We get out to the police cruiser and he opens the back door. I know this is all for show, so I go with it. I get in, and Ben heads around to the driver's seat. "We need to ditch the cruiser," I say to Ben once we're halfway down the road.

"My car is at the station. The last few days have been a clusterfuck."

"Fill me in."

"The FBI showed up earlier this week to let us know of their operation, out of courtesy. I jumped in, wanting to be a part of it when I found out you'd involved yourself with Katsuo Vang. Fuck, Anna, do you have any idea who he is?"

"Yeah, I do. I managed to get into his inner circle."

"They bombarded us, but I couldn't not be part of it. I had to make sure you were okay." He looks over his shoulder at me. "What happened to your face?"

"Don't worry about me, I can handle myself."

"I know you can, but that's not going to stop me from worrying about you."

Aww, how sweet. "Don't be a fucking marshmallow now, Ben. Your sister needs you."

Ben exhales and relaxes against the seat. Until we reach Bankstown Creek, he remains quiet. "I need to go in and get a few things."

"I'll come with you."

"Just so you know, I kept the investigation with the FBI out of the station, but it'll be only a matter of time before they find out. News always travels."

He parks the cruiser and opens the back door for me. Together we head into the station, where I see Grace sitting and typing away on the computer. "Anna," she says surprised. "How are you? I haven't seen you in a while."

My eyes immediately notice her baby bump. "I see things have changed. Congratulations."

The happiness a pregnant woman would usually exude doesn't radiate from Grace. "Thank you," she says in a small voice. I can't help but notice the sadness in her eyes. Is she okay?

Ben goes ahead, and I see a very pretty dark-haired woman approach him. She places her hand on his forearm and smiles at him. What in the actual fuck does she think she's doing? The flames of jealousy blaze through me as I watch her touching my man. I leave Grace and head over to where the brazen brunette is touching something that doesn't belong to her.

"If there's anything I can do," I hear her saying to Ben in her perfect and stupid sing-song voice.

"Adele, this is Anna. Anna, this is my second, Adele."

"Hi." She smiles pleasantly at me, but I don't respond. Instead, I look to where her hand is, and she quickly removes it.

I extend my hand to shake hers. "Anna," I say in a deadpan voice. Don't fucking touch him or I'll tear your fucking arm out of the socket.

"Adele Wilson." She takes my hand in hers and I instantly hate how I don't have the serpent-bite feeling. It means she's not evil and I can't destroy her. Damn it.

"We need to go," I say to Ben as I drop her hand in disappointment.

"Give me a minute, I need to go to my office." I follow him to his office and stand guard, watching Adele as she backs away. *Yeah, thought so.* He's mine, and don't even think about coming close to him again.

"Are you jealous?" Ben asks as he packs his service revolver away.

"Of her? No."

"Funny how you knew who I was talking about." I flick him a look of utter anger. "I'll shut up now."

I look at the clock in his office, then back to Ben. "We need to move."

He closes the top drawer of his desk and walks around to the front. "I'm ready."

As we head out to the front of the station, I can't help but notice how different Grace is. "Congratulations again, Grace," I say.

"Thank you," she replies in a flat tone. She breaks eye contact and lowers her chin to stare at her hands.

We leave the station and get into Ben's car, but I keep an eye on Grace. She wipes at her eyes, then lifts her glass to take a sip of water. "Something is going on with Grace, she looks..." I pause, trying to find the right word. "...sad."

"Sad? What?" I shake my head, pushing Grace's sadness down as far as I can. We have a bigger job on hand and that is to find Claire. "Where are we going?"

"To my cabin."

Ben's brows rise. "Your cabin? But, it was destroyed."

"And rebuilt."

"No, it wasn't. I've been out there."

"New cabin," I say. "It's completely off the grid."

"What the fuck, Anna? Is that where you're staying?"

"Not exactly." That reminds me, I have no need for the other house now. I'll need to call Agent and tell him what to do with it. That house was all for Katsuo's benefit, and *only* his benefit. "What can you tell me about Claire's abduction?"

Ben wets his lips and sucks in a breath. "I think she was taken as a warning to me."

"A warning? Who would want to warn you?" What's he done that warrants someone kidnapping his sister? He opens his mouth to say something, then closes it again. I take these moments to direct him to my rebuilt cabin and decide to not push him any further until we're at the cabin.

"Where is this cabin of yours?" he asks as we make our way down a dirt track.

"Park up there." I point a makeshift clearing. "Wait here." I head into the scrubland and find the small shipping container that blends into its surroundings. There's a fingerprint lock on it, so I press my thumb to it and the lock opens. Inside is an ATV, an array of weapons and ammunition, a first aid kit, a survival backpack, and a camouflaged car cover in case of aerial surveillance.

I search through the backpack and find a GPS phone that's ringing.

"Yeah," I answer as I push the ATV out, then take the car cover.

"Nice to have you back in the land of living, 15. FBI is a pain in the ass, isn't it?"

"They certainly threw a monkey wrench into my plans. But for now, Katsuo has to wait."

"What do you need?"

"Ben and I are heading up to the cabin, I'll be in contact soon." I hang up and place the phone in my back pocket. "Here." The car cover is heavy and I indicate for Ben to help me with it.

"You're an amazing person," Ben says as we pull the cover over his car.

"I'm prepared. Go find some branches with leaves and place them over the car."

Ben wanders off as I start the ATV and wait for him. It doesn't take long before he returns, throwing some lighter branches over his car, and gets on the back of the ATV with me. The ride to the cabin takes only a few minutes. It would've been a good fifteen minutes by foot.

Once inside, I grab two bottles of water from the stocked fridge and hand one to Ben. "Who do you think took Claire?" I ask as I jump up and sit on the kitchen counter. Ben opens the lid of the water bottle and takes a long drink. His resistance in answering the question is a clear indicator he's hiding something. "What aren't you telling me?"

He lowers the bottle and leans against the counter beside me. "Claire's involved with people she shouldn't be and I think they took her to warn me." He's stalling by only giving me limited information.

"Do you want my help, Ben?"

"Of course," he replies instantly.

"Then what aren't you telling me? If you give me only part of what I need, then I'm going into this blind. And I don't do blind. I take the time and do the research so I know what I'm getting into and can plan accordingly. But in this instance, we don't have time. If you want to waste what time we do have, it's going to take me longer to figure out who has her." I throw my hands up in surrender. "If that's the case, you're on your own." I jump off the counter and begin to walk away.

"Anna." Ben pushes off the counter and links his fingers through mine before I can get too far from him.

"Your secret will get us all killed. Starting with your sister."

His jaw tightens as he looks down to the floor and runs his hand through his messy hair. He lifts his chin and looks at me. "She's involved with the mob."

Well. Fuck me. "As in the mafia?" I ask. Ben nods slowly. "Which family?"

"Pace family."

"Pace family?" I think back to the day Katsuo got the call that a shipment of trafficked women and children had been saved by the Pace and James families. If she's involved with the Pace family, then perhaps she's been taken under instructions from Katsuo. But wouldn't he go after the head of the families?

"Would the James family have taken her?" I ask. It could be completely unrelated to what I'm thinking.

"No. They are one of two entities who've joined together."

"Names."

"The Pace and James families," Ben says.

This is looking like Katsuo is behind it. "Go on."

"They joined forces because neither believe in human trafficking. Pace is about the weapons, and James is about moving drugs." Why have I never used Pace? I'll have Agent set up a meeting with them so I can go direct. My current supplier has always been good to me, but it might be time to find a new supply chain. "They heard of a large shipment of women and kids and they intercepted it before they could be trafficked."

"Did Claire tell you who owned the shipment?"

He shakes his head. "There were whispers it was Vang."

"Why take Claire though?" Something isn't adding up. Ben's still hiding something. "What have you got to do with this, Ben?"

"Maybe they need my reach at the station." He shrugs and turns his head away. I can feel something isn't right. He's still keeping things from me.

"I need a minute," I say as I walk away from him. Dad always taught me to breathe through the difficult situations, and that's exactly what I'm going to do. I need a few moments to clear my mind and try to formulate a plan. In these breaths of quiet I start to see a clearer picture of what I need to do. I open my eyes and take my phone out of my pocket. "There's a warehouse I need heat signatures on." I fill Agent in on where the warehouse is. "Also, check all of Katsuo's industrial properties, I need you to tell me if any of them have been accessed in the last forty-eight hours."

"The FBI has run your prints."

"What did they find?"

"Nothing, because I routed them to your Anna Moore profile. And, they won't find anything even if they look, because 15 is a ghost."

"And the earlier requests?"

"All sorted and ready to go on your okay. The information I gained on Takumi..."

"He's been taken care of."

"Of course, he has," Agent chuckles. *Snarky bastard.*

"What about Tyler?"

"A hired mercenary, but I have to say, 15, I'm digging further into him because I wasn't convinced by what I found."

"Keep me updated." I chew on my inner cheek as I keep thinking. "What's the ETA on the information I need about the warehouses?"

"I'm scanning the premises now. I should have the information to you within the next twenty minutes."

I hang up and walk out to Ben. "I think I know who has Claire."

"Who?" Ben asks. "Where is she?"

"I don't know the location yet, but I suspect Katsuo's men have taken her."

"We have to go." He rushes toward the door, but I stay put. He turns and sees me standing still. "Come on, Anna, we have to go."

"What are you going to do, start knocking on doors? I said I think I know who has her, not where she is. Agent's working on it now and he'll have a location within the next twenty minutes."

Ben paces back and forth in front of the door. "The more time we sit here doing nothing—"

"Stop." I walk over to him and throw my arms around his waist. This is the first moment we've been able to be with each other all day. A moment where we can decompress and breathe. "You have to trust me, because this is what I do. Rushing out with only part of the solution won't get you anywhere, and it could essentially get Claire and you killed. Especially if they think we're onto them. If it is Katsuo who has her, he'd kill her and not have a second thought about it."

"I know but I'm worried." He presses a kiss to the top of my head.

"You have to trust that I know what I'm doing."

Ben runs his hands up and down my back while squeezing our bodies together. "I do trust you."

My phone rings, and I step back, breaking our contact. "Yeah," I say as I answer it.

"There are two locations where I've breached the security feed. One has a woman held in a small dungeon-like room; the other premises…" he pauses. Jesus, how bad is it that Agent is struggling to tell me? "Has a young girl. *Very* young, 15…"

There's a pounding in my ears as adrenaline rushes through my veins. "Are they using her?" I ask through a clenched jaw.

Agent intakes a long breath and sighs. "Yeah."

"Names and images of every person who's touched that little girl." My tone is low and controlled. I look over to Ben, whose forehead is creased as he steps toward me. I shake my head at him.

"15—"

"Have Doctor on standby for the little girl. I want you to give that property up to every government agency within the hour. I want them raided, today. Get that kid anything she needs."

"I'll take care of it."

My breathing is sharp and ragged; I need to control myself before I lose my shit. "Send me the address where the woman is. How many men are in and around the building?"

"There are four and I'll stay hacked into the feed. Also, Katsuo is still held up and there's no release date or time for him. He won't be arraigned until late this afternoon, and we need to assume he'll get bail. You have a small window to get her out before he returns."

"Is there a laptop in the weapons room?"

"There is," Agent confirms.

I walk over to the room and with my fingerprint, the reinforced steel door opens. "Get me a live feed into the building she's in." I open the laptop and wait for him to get the feed on the screen. I need to confirm the woman being held is indeed Claire, if it isn't, I'll have Agent tip off all the authorities on where she is so they can go in and save her.

"Connecting you now."

The screen flicks to the live feed. I toggle between different cameras and come to the one with the woman in the cage. I take my laptop out to Ben. "Is this Claire?" I turn the screen so he can see.

Ben takes in a sharp breath as his jaw relaxes and his mouth turns down. That's all the confirmation I need. It's his sister. "Fuck," he whispers. He lifts his hand and clutches at his chest, but his eyes are glued to the screen where he can see Claire balled into the corner, with her head turned up. "What have they done to her?" He turns and walks away while shaking his head. "Jesus," he groans a low and painful cry.

I give him a moment to worry for his sister, but any more than that is wasted time. "You're no good to anyone in this state," I finally say.

He looks to me with deep crinkles in his forehead as he runs his hands through his hair. "I'm going to fucking kill him."

"No, you're not." Ben flexes his fingers before balling them into fists. "Katsuo's death will be long and drawn out. I know he's hurt your sister, and anyone in your position would want to make sure he pays for that." I step closer to him and tenderly place my hand on his heaving chest. "But he dies by my hand because he owes me."

Ben visibly gulps and purses his lips together. "He owes us both his life."

"I can't let him die quickly. He has to hurt, for everything he's done."

Ben swallows hard and obviously while taking a step backward. His aversion to allowing me to take care of Katsuo is evident, but I can't let anyone else kill Katsuo. "Maybe," he mutters.

"There's no maybe, Ben. I'll get her out alive, because this is a hit for freedom. Claire's and all those women and kids he traffics for monetary reward. I have to end this."

Ben's resistance is quickly fading as he understands my need to finish Katsuo, once and for all. He finally relinquishes and nods. "Promise me you'll get her out alive, and you can have him. I don't care what you do to him. I just want my sister out."

My phone rings before I get a chance to respond. I sit on the armchair and place the laptop on my knees. "Yeah," I answer.

"The FBI are holding him for another thirty-hours maximum. Katsuo's lawyers are attempting to secure bail but the DA is saying he's a flight risk and trying to revoke his passport before they allow bail which will be set at twenty-five million."

"Fuck," I grumble. Twenty-five million is pocket change for Katsuo, not to mention he travels by private jet everywhere so leaving the country would be as easy as breathing.

"There's more you should know."

"What?" I humorless chuckle escapes my throat.

"The good news is the industrial building where the little girl is being kept in is about to be raided. Doctor's on standby, and we secured her a temporary foster family that takes in kids with trauma. I'm working on tracking her actual family down, but until her prints come up in the system, I don't have much to go on. I've also secured one of the best psychologists at dealing with childhood trauma to be at the hospital for her."

"Finally, a government agency that works quickly." At least that's something positive.

"I've also reviewed the security video feeds from the building and I've identified three men who've—"

"Don't say it," I warn. Those acts are the worst of the worst. They make my stomach churn with anger. "Just get me their pictures and tell me where I can find them."

"I'll send them over to you. And I'll send you a blueprint of the building too."

"Good."

"There's more."

"Fuck's sake," I grumble. "What is it now?"

"The mole at Bankstown Creek PD."

I look to Ben and intake a deep breath. Ben keeps his eyes on me. "You know who's leaking information from Ben's department?"

Ben steps closer and mouths, *who?*

"It's not a cop. It's Grace Campbell."

"Grace?" I repeat. "Are you sure?"

"Have I ever been wrong?"

"Grace?" Ben asks with the same amount of disbelief as I'm holding. "How...?"

"Vang made a phone call to his lawyer. I tapped the lawyer's phone. He asked him to reach out to the mole at the station to gather whatever information he could on Ben."

"Ben?" I ask. "My Ben?" I lift my gaze to look at Ben.

"Yeah."

"And how do you know it's Grace?"

"I did some digging around. Vang or one of his men had Grace's husband murdered in front of her and they threatened to kill her unborn child."

Just when I thought I couldn't hate him any more than I do, I'm proven wrong. "What do they know about Ben?"

"At this stage, I'm not sure because Grace hasn't responded to Vang's demand."

I hang up, place the laptop on the coffee table, and stand from the armchair. "That man is venomous and needs to be a head shorter." He makes me fucking sick. He's proven to me time and time again that he'll destroy any life as long as he gets what he wants. "Call your other sister and tell her to get out of wherever they are. Take no phones, and only use cash. Claire's married, right?"

"Both of my sisters are."

"Call Claire's husband and tell him the same thing. Tell them to purchase disposable phones and give them this number." I head into the kitchen to find a note pad and pen in my third drawer and write the number of my phone down. "They need to get to a safe location, somewhere completely off the grid. And make sure to tell them to make no phone calls other than to this number." I thrust the paper at Ben. "Only this number," I reiterate. I hand him the phone.

"I'll make the calls outside. I need to clear my head."

"Okay, take your time." Ben leaves the cabin to make his calls. I can hear muffled talking, but nothing clear enough for me to make out. I pull up the blueprints Agent has sent over and concentrate on the floor plan so I know where I'm going. This needs to be fast and clean, and I need to get her out before they realize I'm there for her.

I can easily take out the security already on hand, but if Katsuo gets wind of anyone coming for Claire, he'll increase the security and that may hinder me getting to her. I look outside and see Ben pacing back and forth as he runs his hand through his hair. He stops walking and lowers his hand to point in front of him. He shakes his head numerous times, then begins pacing again. He stops once more and nods. I see he pulls the phone away from his ear and ends the call. Ben stands outside for another moment before finally pulling his shoulders back and entering the cabin. The moment our eyes meet, his shoulders slump down. "They want to fight."

"Don't let them. They're not trained, and I can't be watching them and getting your sister out at the same time."

"I'm coming with you," he says.

"Yeah, you are." I know Ben will take the shot, I'm not so sure his sister and brothers-in-law would. Ben's tense jaw and the dark circles beneath his eyes tell me he's at breaking point. "You're running on fumes. We need to have something to eat and go to bed, because tomorrow will be a long day."

"I can't sleep knowing my sister is chained up like a rabid dog."

"This is what we know, Ben. Katsuo wants information on you which means he's not going to do anything to your sister until he knows where you are. He also has no idea we've got a live feed into the warehouse where she's being kept, nor is he in any position to go anywhere because he's still being detained by the FBI. She's not going anywhere, and neither are we. Not until we both get food and sleep. Because neither of us can get to her if our heads aren't clear."

"How do you do it?"

"Do what?"

"Remain so calm when the situation is disastrous?"

"Because I'm damn good at what I do, and I know that no matter what happens, I'm always in control."

"Even when it's personal?"

"Especially when it's personal. I killed the man who tried to take me, and it took me thirteen years to get to him. But I got to him, and I didn't bat an eye when I did. I also killed my mother." Ben's brows rise. "My own mother."

"I'd say you're a cold-hearted person, but I know you're not. You have morals and standards and aren't..." He runs his hands through his hair as he lowers his chin.

"Psychotic?" I fill in the blank. "I don't go around killing people who don't deserve it."

"You're amazing."

"I'm a criminal," I reply. "But, I'm good at what I do."

"Have you ever thought about not being an assassin?"

There's a long drawn out and tense silence. "Since I was forced into this business, I've never really thought of getting out."

"There's going to come a time, though, that you won't be able to keep doing this."

I take my bottle of water from the kitchen counter, open it, and take a long drink. "The demons will come for me one day, and when they do, my time will be up."

Ben's brows furrow together as he tilts his head to the side. "You think you'll be killed on the job?"

"I have no idea." I shrug. "But I do know that people like me don't go out by falling asleep and never waking up again. I've killed too many people and owe too many debts to die a peaceful death."

"Fuck." Ben clicks his tongue to the roof of his mouth. "Then get out now and make it right so you don't die under those circumstances."

"I told you, I'm prepared to meet my maker. And I'm at peace with that."

He leans against the kitchen counter and crosses his arms in front of his chest. "This is fucked."

"This is my life," I correct. "Anyway, I'm going to take a shower while you make us something to eat."

"Designated chef, am I?" Ben jokes, but rounds the counter to start rummaging around in the kitchen. "There's nothing fresh." He looks over to me waiting for a reply. I simply shrug. "I'll figure it out."

I begin stripping before I'm even in the bedroom, and I'm totally nude by the time I reach the bathroom. I turn on the water and step under the stream once it's up to temperature.

I feel like I'm in the middle of a giant puzzle and some pieces are hidden from me. What am I missing? What's the common thread holding it all together that I'm not seeing?

The FBI are holding Katsuo, for now. Check.

Grace is Katsuo's informer from Bankstown Creek Police Department. Check.

Katsuo wants information on Ben. But why?

Is there still another dirty cop at Bankstown Creek? Or is Grace the only rat?

And of course, Claire is being held by Katsuo because of her involvement of his missing shipment.

"What the fuck can't I see?" I smack my hand against the wall in frustration.

Wait, Tyler told me to leave before the raid. Did he know about it? The more I think about it, the more I'm convinced he knew the raid was coming. How?

I don't know; something isn't adding up. This is screwing with my head. I hate not being able to see the big picture. I despise surprises, especially when so many of the possible outcomes are deadly.

I turn the shower off and dry myself. Once dressed, I head out to the kitchen where Ben is standing over the range stirring something. He turns toward me and startles. "Shit, you need a damn bell."

I chuckle as I stealthily walk into the kitchen and peek at what he's making. "Spaghetti?"

"With red sauce. You have no ground beef, or chicken, or any kind of protein, so it's vegetarian."

"Smells good," I say.

"You don't have much to work with here."

"My houses are stocked with quick and easy meal options that have a long shelf life. I never know where I'm going to be, so it makes sense."

"Who does all of this for you?" He gestures around the kitchen.

"Agent takes care of it. He knows how I like things, so he does what I need him to do."

Ben strains the spaghetti before dividing it into two bowls and spooning the sauce over them. "Here you go." He places the two bowls down next to each other at the counter and grabs two bottles of water from the fridge.

I sit and twirl my spaghetti onto the fork but I notice he's pushing his around as he stares ahead. "You're worried," I say.

"Aren't you?"

A part of me is, only because I'm still not aware of all the variables involved in saving Claire. But, if I show him weakness, Ben might lose confidence in me and do something stupid. "Not at all," I lie. "I know I can get her out."

"I know you can too, but I'm worried that between now and tomorrow that anything can happen."

"Anything can happen," I say. "But, I'm good at what I do, Ben. I've never missed a target in my life, and I don't plan on starting now."

He twirls some spaghetti and pops it in his mouth. It's easy to see he's thinking and stressed. "You've never missed a target?" he asks slowly.

"Why do you think they come to me when they need a difficult job done? I can hit a target from miles away."

He shakes his head and stares down at his mostly untouched bowl of food. "I'm worried, Anna." I place my hand over his and give him a gentle squeeze. "But, I'm glad it's you and me going in there to get her. I don't trust anyone else to save her. And, I know we'll take down anyone who'll stand in our way."

"You better believe it." It might be time to tell Ben the plan. At least it will set his mind at ease. I stand and grab the laptop. Opening it, I place it on the counter between us and pull up the blueprints. "We're hitting them early in the morning."

"Okay."

"See here?" I open another tab on the laptop and bring up an aerial image of the warehouse. I point to the south side and say, "This is how I'm going in, because Claire is being held here." I flick between the aerial and the blueprint. "I'll set up my rifle here, about seven hundred yards out and take out the guards positioned here and here." I point to the exterior where the guards are. "We'll set up eyes here and here, and here." I point to all the crucial points of the building. "You'll need to stay focused and keep me informed of all the guards' locations. I'll take out as many as I can, but this has to be lightning-fast, because once they call for backup, we're on borrowed time. I want to get in and out before they have any idea what's hit them."

"I need to be the one to get her, Anna."

"You'll slow me down, and you may end up getting Claire and me both killed."

"No," he replies adamantly. "I'm coming in with you."

My stomach churns with what I have to do, but if I don't, this mission will be a failure. Anna Brookes is taken over by 15. I pull my shoulders back and sneer toward him. "If you think I'm going to let you fuck this up and get me killed, then you're on your own. You go get her, and see how far you'll get."

Ben stares at me. "I can't believe how arrogant you are. She's my damn sister."

"And the only way she's going to come out of this alive is if I get her."

Ben suddenly stands and paces back and forth. He drags his fingers through his hair while muttering to himself. He stops pacing and turns to me. "I'm coming with you," he says as if his word is final.

Fuck this shit. I stand and match his energy, going toe–to-toe with him. He may be taller than me, but I can put him on his ass easily. I poke my finger into his chest and look him dead in the eyes. "You're no good to me. You can stay here and wait."

"No. What?" Ben's eyes widen. "This is my fucking family. My sister!"

"You're not capable of killing all those men and saving your sister. No negotiation, Ben. If you can't follow my rules, you're not coming. Or you can do it yourself. Those are your only options. Choose one."

"I..."

I throw my hands up and walk to the door. "You've made your choice, get out and good luck."

"You don't have to be in control all the time, Anna."

"Yeah, I do. It's the only way we all survive this. It's my way or you can fuck off and try it your way." I open the door wider. "Good luck," I repeat. "You're gonna need it."

It takes Ben all of a minute to figure out that without me, he has no chance of getting Claire out. His shoulders instantly droop forward and he releases a long sigh. "I can't do this without you."

"I know, but I can. I told you, we're doing this my way, or you can leave now."

He walks over and closes the door. "I'll do whatever it takes to get my sister back." He steps into my personal space and wraps his arms around me. "Whatever it takes," he whispers as he kisses me on the side of the head.

Ben relinquishes his control over to me. It's what's needed if there's any chance of getting Claire out alive. This isn't for the faint of heart. "We need to get ready for bed," I say.

With his arms still wrapped around me, and our dinner long forgotten, we head into the bedroom. "Come here," he says as he lies back and opens his arms.

I coil into his warmth and rest my head on his chest.

Tomorrow will be like no job I've ever done before. Although personal, I now have a partner I need to worry about. I'm worried I'm going to get Ben killed. But I don't speak the words to him.

I can't lose Ben.

Fuck. I think I may be falling for him.

Fuck.

CHAPTER FIFTEEN

— ◆ —

ANNA

The alarm should've woken me, but I've been awake since three. I have a feeling Ben hasn't slept a wink at all.

Silently, Ben and I stand from the bed and dress. I wear my all-black attire, military boots, fitted tights, and a sweater. I pull my hair back into a tight ponytail and mentally prepare myself for what's going to happen.

Once Ben is dressed, he heads out of the bedroom. This gives me a moment to rein in my uncertainty and hone my control.

I sit on the bed and close my eyes. I concentrate on nothing but my breathing. I relax my body, calm my pulse, and center myself. A chill of excitement runs through my body while goose bumps prickle my arms. I can hear every sound close to me.

A bat flaps its wings as it flies over head.

Ben clears his throat in the kitchen before the faucet is turned on.

The leaves in the trees outside rustle as a slight breeze passes between them.

In this moment, I'm not Anna Moore. I'm a ruthless killer who will destroy anyone in my path. I'll get Claire back and make sure Ben is safe. I snap my eyes open with razor focus. The only people who'll die today are Katsuo's men.

I take in another deep breath and release it. Utter calm flows through me.

I stand and make my way out to my weapons room. "Ben," I say.

"Yeah."

"Choose your weapons."

I grab one of the duffels and start packing my weapons into it. I also grab hand grenades and surveillance equipment. I look at my guns and smile. "Hello," I say as I pick my favorite hand guns up. I check the ammunition, then pack more.

"You have sniper rifles."

"Yes," I reply coldly as I take the partially disassembled Barrett and pack it into the duffel.

"You're lethal with these weapons, Anna."

I look over to Ben and crinkle my brows. "I'm lethal without them too."

"You haven't divulged much about your training. How deadly are you exactly?"

"Extremely."

"Could you kill someone without a weapon?"

"Yes," I reply honestly. "Both quickly and slowly."

"Huh," he huffs. "You're fucking terrifying."

"Only if you do me wrong." I click my tongue to the roof of my mouth. "Or if I'm paid."

"You were paid to kill me, but you didn't."

"You're an anomaly." He looks over to me, silently questioning my reply. "I could've killed you. I actually had planned on it, but..."

"But what?" he pushes.

"It turns out I've grown fond of you. So, I figured I'd keep you around for a while."

"A while?"

"Who knows, you might piss me off."

Ben stares at me, his face completely impassive. It takes him a moment before the corner of his lip lifts into a smirk. "Note to self—stay on your good side." He returns his attention to the weapons and picks a semi-automatic and two handguns to take with him.

Once finished with the weapon selection, I take the duffel out of the weapons room and grab my phone. I dial Agent. "I need Doctor and Cleaner on standby near the building where the woman's held."

"Already done, 15. I've been monitoring the FBI and Vang is still in custody. They're trying to hold him for several more days." Several days will work for what I need to do. "There are four guards at the building now, but I can't see any other change happening, so you're good to go this morning."

"Good."

"Also, Doctor examined the girl and has given his recommendations to the hospital. The three men who were there at the time have been taken into custody, and they're being held until their hearing. No one's come to bail them out, do you want me to arrange bail so you can take care of them?"

"Not yet. Let me get the woman out and then we'll look at posting their bail."

"The paperwork you had me fabricate for the men at the meeting table is ready to go, when you give me the go-ahead, I'll send it to the FBI and CIA. All of them will be charged with embezzlement and fraud. It'll make enough of a racket to take them all down and send a message to other Yakuza. When we're through with them, the entire operation will be shut down because they'll be hot on the FBI and CIA most wanted lists for a while. They'll have no choice but to leave the country and take their businesses with them."

"It's ironclad, right?" I ask Agent. "I want them gone."

"There's no way the FBI and CIA won't jump at what I've given them and tear them down. Besides, the FBI have been after them for years. Now they'll get them."

"Send the information once Katsuo has been released."

Agent snickers. "He has no idea the pain he's going to be in. Every single thing points to him fucking over the Yakuza. He'll go into hiding if they don't get to him first."

"I'll kill him before they do."

"I'm keeping an eye on the warehouse, and I'll let you know if anything changes."

I hang up and turn to find Ben. He's sipping on a coffee while staring blankly at the floor in front of him. Absentmindedly, he rubs at the back of his neck. His foot is rapidly tapping on the ground. Ben's nervous, and for good reason too. We're about to go and rescue his sister. I guess if I had a sister I liked, I'd be worried too. But, I don't have a sister, and the one person I did love was stolen from me when I was fifteen.

I walk over to him and place my hand on his forearm. "I've got this," I say.

"I know," he replies, but the sincerity is forced. I know he wants to believe that I'm going to get her out alive, but he's freaking out over something that hasn't happened.

"I've got this," I repeat, firmer. He looks over to me and offers me a tight smile to hide his worry. "Let's go over the plan once more so you know what to do."

"Okay."

I grab the laptop so I can tell him the attack plan step-by-step. "Once we're there, you need to remain stealth. Our only form of communication will be through the comms. And you only use them if absolutely needed. I'll have you and Agent in my ear at the same time."

Ben nods his acknowledgement. "I know what to do."

I glance at him and can feel the tension radiating off of him. "Keep your emotions in check, and we'll be fine. If you lose your cool, you may as well take that gun and put a bullet in your head because you'll sign all our death warrants."

"I know," he replies.

I sweep the cabin one last time and gesture toward the duffel. Ben lifts it and follows me out of the house. Although I'm confident in my abilities, there's still something hanging over me. I know I'm missing something. I just need to figure out what it is. I look to Ben and know in my gut that this may very well be the last time I see him.

I might die going into this. I know Claire and Ben will get out of this relatively unscathed. I can't be so sure about myself though. Considering I don't know all the variables yet. My skin prickles as a quiver trembles though my chest. I close the door and turn to Ben and fist his shirt into my hands. I drag him down and smash our mouths together.

Ben releases the duffel and snakes his hands on my hips, gripping them tightly while we share what could possibly be our very last kiss. I push my body into his, silently speaking the words I can't say.

I hate having to pull away from our connection, but I know it has to happen. "Are you okay?" Ben asks without letting my body go.

I clear my throat and step back. "We have a job to do." And I might never see you again.

"Yeah, we do." Ben takes a step forward toward me but I lift my hand to stop him. "Okay," he says. "Okay." Ben grabs the duffel bag and straightens his shoulders.

I place my earphone in and dial Agent. "You're all good to go. Nothing has changed. I've secured a truck and it's at the drop-off point."

"Good." I jump on the ATV and start it. Ben saddles up behind me with the duffel slung across his back.

Once we arrive where we left Ben's car, there's a black truck waiting for us. I check the rear wheel well and find the fob for keyless entry. Ben shakes his head and snickers. "I'm not even surprised."

"About what?"

"A truck magically turns up here. The reach you have to make something like this happen must be extraordinary."

"Agent is good at his job."

"Obviously." He points to the truck. "Can he get you anything?"

"With deep enough pockets, nearly everything is possible."

"How deep are your pockets?" he cheekily asks.

I heave myself up in the truck and wait until he's in. "Fucking deep."

The drive to the warehouse is silent as Ben and I are getting into the right headspace. I get Ben to the drop-off point. I grab his arm before he exits the truck. "You know where to meet and you know what to do."

"I do."

"We need ears and eyes at the rear. You have..." I look at my watch, then back to Ben. "...thirty-three minutes."

He leans over and places one last kiss to my mouth before leaving by foot.

I watch as he disappears into the landscape under the cover of darkness before I head to where I need to be. The truck is concealed by large birch trees, making it nearly impossible to be seen. I get out of the truck, lift the rifle, and set it up about five hundred yards from the truck.

There's a damp frost blanketing the ground and the air around me is cold and unforgiving. I lie on the ground and peer through the scope. I open the laptop beside me and see Ben's managed to set up one of the cameras. I can hear him through the earpiece. His breath is quick as he runs from one position to the next.

I watch as the second camera comes to life. "I have one more to set up," he whispers.

His breath quickens again, and I can hear the sound of the crunchy frost beneath his boots as he runs toward the third section. *Come on, you can do this.* I check the laptop, waiting for a visual from the third camera. "Where are you?"

The laptop splits into three sections giving me a clear view of the building. "I'm heading over."

He has less than fifteen minutes to travel the one-point-three miles over to me. We're running on borrowed time before the sun breaks over the horizon and Ben's seen. I watch the cameras in case there's a change while I wait for Ben to approach. I close my eyes for a moment, to heighten my hearing. I hear the rustle of the frost-stiffened ground beneath his boots. But I'm not taking any chances. I turn to my back and aim both of my Glocks at whoever's coming at me. I hold my breath and keep a laser focus ahead.

"It's me," Ben whispers as he comes into view.

I holster my weapons and turn to look through the scope again. The sun is just peeking out over the horizon. I watch and monitor the men who are standing around outside. There's one who's doing a perimeter walk-around, while three are standing around smoking and talking. There's a part of me that's happy I don't see Tyler. He was decent to me, and I may have hesitated for a second in killing him.

Maybe.

Probably not.

But I might've been conflicted.

Maybe.

I look at the laptop again. "Just like last time, tap me on the shoulder if you see danger. But we need to be silent from here on in."

Ben nods and takes in a deep breath.

I close my eyes and breathe in and out. All I need to do is concentrate and breathe.

My eyes snap open and I take one last deep breath before looking through the scope of my rifle. The three targets are still standing together. The fourth is approaching from the far side.

Wait, 15. Wait for them to be closer together. Closer, target four, come closer.

Come on, move toward your buddies. I need you to be together.

Shit, one of three breaks away and heads toward the door.

I can't wait until they're together. My finger depresses the trigger. The bullet leaves the barrel and target four, the one closest to the door, is down. I slightly swivel the rifle and get the other three in my scope. They all look to the one that's down and pause in shock for a moment before they start yelling at one another.

The second shot takes out target one.

The other two startle backward and look around searching for me. I take out the third guy only leaving me with one more target. He dives behind the dumpster, but I can't see him. "Fuck," I grumble. No, wait. The tip of his foot is sticking out. That'll get him out from behind the dumpster. Another bullet leaves my barrel and blows his left foot off. His shriek echoes through the woods. I can't help but snicker at his hysterical cries of agony. He heaves forward to grab at his ankle giving me the opportunity I need. I take the next shot, and within seconds his head explodes. "Thank you," I say to my rifle before jumping to my feet and turning to Ben. "Pack my rifle and get yourself to the truck. Take the laptop and monitor it. If anything happens, get yourself out of here and return to the cabin. I'll get Claire and meet you there."

"How will you get back?"

"I've got it covered, Ben," Agent says.

Ben hesitates for a moment but proceeds with what I've asked him to do. I'm just about to take off toward the building but Ben reaches out and takes my hand in his. He pulls me back and presses a kiss to my lips. "Come back to me," he whispers. Ben strokes my cheek and kisses me again.

"I will." My steps falter because I want to say more to Ben, but now's not the time. I pull my shoulders back and look at the laptop. "Keep an eye on that." I point to my earpiece. "But remember, quiet."

"I got it."

With all the guards now down, I need to remain stealthy because we don't know if eyes are still watching the building. Once I'm at the warehouse, I draw my weapons, ready to go in and rescue Claire. My back is against the wall, and I take a moment to control my breathing. Years of discipline have allowed me to be able to conquer any hint of nerves.

But this is different. It's a rescue mission, not a hit. God, I wish Katsuo was here so I could show him exactly who he's up against. I'd set Claire free and tell her to wait for Ben, then I'd take my time hurting Katsuo. I'd start with his extremities and slowly make my way through the rest of his body. I'd make him cry and beg, and just when he couldn't take any more, I'd pump him high with adrenaline and start all over again.

Nothing would bring me greater pleasure than torturing Katsuo. *Nothing.*

Although I wish he was here, I know he's not. And this is a hit for Claire's freedom. I place my hand on the door knob but Agent and Ben both scream, "Run!" The word alone is innocent, however both Ben's and Agent's shrieks are terrifying. Their high pitch and sheer volume tells me I'm in trouble.

Adrenaline chokes my veins while my throat starts to tighten.

"It's a trap," Agent repeats louder.

For a split second, I completely freeze. Unable to get my legs to move. "Run!" Ben hollers. With my weapons in my hands, I turn and start flat out running toward the trees where my truck is. "I'm coming."

"No, get out of here!" I call to him as I run with everything I have. Fucking Katsuo set a trap. How did we not see this? Where the fuck is Claire? "Get back to the cabin."

Agent is screaming in my ear. The words are jumbled yet desperate. Suddenly, the ground beneath my boots vibrates, forcing me to lose my footing. A massive explosion catapults me forward. My body protests in pain, but I try—unsuccessfully—to move.

My ears are ringing and I'm lying face down on the unrelenting ground. A warm, metallic fluid fills my mouth. I groan as I attempt to crawl away, but my torso forces me to crumple in pain.

I manage to drag my legs under my body to stand, but everything inside of me is gripped with agony. My brain is screaming at me to move, but my body is refusing to cooperate. It feels like hours pass when I finally manage to turn my head and see the building is in an absolute inferno. The fire ravages the walls, licking them with ferocity as it engulfs everything it touches.

I failed. I couldn't save Claire. There's no way she survived this. I fucking failed. An innocent died because of me. *Fuck.*

Black dots dance in front of me as I struggle to keep my eyes open.

I fight the darkness calling me, but it's getting stronger with each heartbeat.

I suck in a breath as I blink my eyelids open, but the black haze takes over.

Someone chuckles as I'm easily picked up. "I should be surprised," the voice says. "But I'm not."

A calm weightlessness showers me. Fight it, Anna. Open your fucking eyes. I will myself to comply, but my body is refusing to listen to my demands. "Let me go!" I scream at whoever is carrying me. But my voice isn't leaving my body. Shit, shit, what's happening?

Darkness finally wins and claims me.

Fuck.

CHAPTER SIXTEEN

—·—

ANNA

Tap.

Tap, tap.

Tap.

My eyes struggle to open so I keep them closed. I can hear the whir of a slow ceiling fan. Then a scrape of a chair against a hard floor. There are people in the distance talking about something, but I can't quite make out what they're saying.

Open your eyes.

I try again, but the blackness is too strong for me. Damn you, I won't let you win.

Black.

"Anna," I hear a woman calling. I look around to see who's calling me, but she's too far away and I can't see her clearly. She reminds me of someone though. "Fight it, don't let them take you. You're stronger than this." Who is she? Who's going to take me?

The black creeps over again, threatening to claim me. No, no! Fuck off, you can't be here. I need to fight this.

Not again.

My mouth hurts when I try to swallow. It feels like I've been feasting on sand and salt water. I lick my lips trying to moisten them, but they're dry too. My eyes flutter open and I try to focus. There's not one part of my body that doesn't ache or feel heavy. I can't even lift my arms; they feel like they're weighted by stone.

"Where am I?" I ask as I keep attempting to focus.

"She's waking," an unfamiliar voice says. I wait for a response from someone so I can figure out where I am and who's around me.

I blink several more times and finally focus. "Where am I?" I look around and see a man dressed in black staring at me. *Shit.* My memory of what happened is fuzzy, but glimpses are coming back to me.

The man stands and walks to the foot of the bed where I notice my legs are restrained. I try my arms and find they too are cuffed. The man draws his weapon and points it at me.

I swallow a few times to wet my mouth but keep my focus on him. "I'm strapped in," I say as he lifts his gun further to point it at my head. Seriously, the guy is an idiot. He must be on the bottom of the totem pole. The one who's paid the least. Katsuo must be scraping the bottom of the barrel if my babysitter feels threatened enough to aim a gun at me while I'm incapacitated.

Shit, that means Katsuo knows who I am.

Double fuck.

I look around the room and don't recognize it from anywhere I've been with Katsuo. The door opens and another guard waltzes in followed by Katsuo.

Tyler's absence is noticeable. Is he alive or dead?

Katsuo shoves his hands into his pockets and glances over at the security he walked in the room with. "Anna Moore, it's good to see you again."

He said Anna Moore, which means he still doesn't know who I really am. "How long have I been out?"

"Four days." He waltzes over to the chair and drags it over toward the bed. The screeching sound of the legs against the floor makes the hair on the back of my neck stand to attention. "What were you doing at the building, Anna?"

I hold his stare for a moment before turning my head and looking up at the peeling ceiling. The paint is flaking off and it's a discolored, dirty shade of yellow. The room crackles with tension as Katsuo waits for my response. I ignore him.

"What were you doing there?" he repeats in a lower, more menacing voice. If a menacing voice is all it takes for me to crack, I'd be a shit assassin. I remain quiet and take in a long, bored breath. Katsuo leaps forward and wraps his cold fingers around my neck. He begins to apply pressure, slowly cutting off my air supply. "Why were you there?"

I don't try to fight it, I go with it. Katsuo can't kill me because he's an egocentric narcissist who demands answers and to be in control. Killing me would leave more unanswered questions than he's prepared for. I flick him a look of condescension and smirk as his fingers tighten further.

Katsuo knows this too and releases. I cough and splutter as I take in deep breaths, but I don't break.

"I asked you a question."

I arch a brow and smirk. "Sleepwalking."

He balls his hand into a fist and punches me in the jaw. "What were you doing there?"

"Big man," I say and look up. The pain in my jaw radiates through my face. "Beating up a woman while she's tied up. Good for you, you hero," I antagonize.

"You're going to end up like your friend, Claire Pace. I knew if I captured one of the heads of the Pace family, then at least her brother would come after her. Fucking family. But no. You came instead."

What did I just hear?

"Who's Claire Pace?" I ask with borderline disinterest, hoping he gives me more information.

"The Pace family caused me to lose millions in revenue when they fucked up that shipment. Not to mention they're causing me more problems with their import and export of artillery. A fucking family of influence. I killed one half of them, and I needed the brother to kill him too." He grits his teeth together. "Now, I need to find the brother and kill him."

Ben is Ben Pace?

I never got that serpent-bite feeling when I touched him. Agent never found anything on him. He was clean. He's not an arms dealer. He can't be.

My stomach churns as I keep staring up at the ceiling. This can't be. He would've told me. He wouldn't have kept something like this from me, not after I told him who I was. I could've killed him. I... Wait.

That's why the Mancinis were willing to pay so much to kill him.

I release a forceful breath as Ben's betrayal hits me with a thousand knives. My hands ball into fists as my entire body stiffens. There's a sharp pain in the base of my throat as I blink rapidly while I attempt to make sense of this.

No, I refuse to believe it. Katsuo is manipulating me; he wants a reaction and I refuse to give it to him. I close my mouth and take in a few sharp breaths through my nose. "Fucking liar," I say as I turn to Katsuo. "You'll say whatever you want to get your way."

"You had no idea you were fucking the enemy, did you?"

I look toward his crotch, then back up to his steely and hard eyes. "It's better than fucking a guy with a pencil dick."

He sneers, then spits at me. "Ben Pace is the enemy here, not me."

Ben's betrayal is devastating. He's blindsided and wounded me all in one fell swoop. I did something I've never done before; I let myself become vulnerable to him and he betrayed my trust.

Why does it feel like my heart is breaking?

I shared my real self with Ben, and he refused to show me the same courtesy. I gave myself to him, let him into my deepest and darkest secrets, and he fooled me. Am I nothing more than a con to him? Did I mean nothing to him?

The bed dips beside me, and I turn to see Katsuo sitting on the edge. He's holding a syringe that he flicks a couple of times. I know what that dirty amber liquid is. Katsuo turns to his guard, who swaps the syringe for a rubber tourniquet. "You'll like this," Katsuo says as he ties the tourniquet around my upper arm. He slaps my arm several times. "You've made me some money, so thank you."

He turns and takes the syringe and flicks it once more. "I'll find you, Katsuo, and I'm going to hurt you."

He snorts as he inserts the needle into my arm. "You're going to a place that there's no coming back from."

"Keep looking over your shoulder." I return his cold and empty sneer.

"Good luck with that," he says as he empties the contents of the syringe into my arm. I know what this is. Dirty fucking heroin. The warmth hits my arm and travels through my body. "Turn her on her side, we don't want the goods dying before she reaches her new home." Katsuo's men laugh as they loosen the bonds on the left and turn me on my side.

"I found you once, I'll find you again," I warn. Katsuo laughs again. Fucker knows I'm in no state to destroy him.

"You could've kept her here and let us all use her," one of his men says.

"If you want to pay me what I'm getting for her, we'll keep her."

"Can I have a taste first?"

These fuckers are dirty and I'm going to take great satisfaction in slitting their throats when the time comes. But for now, I let go and give myself to the drug.

"She's definitely a beauty," I hear someone say. I'm not sure how much time has lapsed since I was injected.

"She's yours to do with as you please." My head is fuzzy and filled with a drug-induced fog. I know there are more people around me. I just can't focus on who they are. "She'll be coming down soon."

"I've got what she needs."

"Remember the deal. If he comes for her, you need to call me."

"I know, mate. It's all good," the man speaks with a foreign accent. "Let's top you up, buttercup, and get you back to the house." Someone smacks my arm and I feel the sting of the needle. That damn warmth overtakes me again forcing my body to relax. Someone easily picks me up and throws me over their shoulder. "She's gonna earn her price back in no time. Just look at this tight ass." Someone grabs my ass and squeezes. "Get her in the van."

"Yes, sir," the reply comes from someone else with a thick foreign accent. I can't quite make out the origin of the accent.

My body is thrown into the back of a van and someone turns me on my side. "We don't need her dead before we leave the country. Fuck, could you imagine?"

"She'd fucking kill us if we brought back someone they paid so much for already dead. I value my balls way too much."

"Keep an eye on her."

Who the fuck are these people? It doesn't matter. I'm going to find each and every one of them and destroy them.

Slowly.

And painfully.

15 is not someone to be messed with.

Armor up, fuckers. I'll be coming for you.

Chapter Seventeen

Ben

"Run!" Agent yells. "It's a trap."

My heart leaps into my throat as I take off toward the building. "Run!" I scream as I make my way toward her. "I'm coming." I've got to get to Anna and Claire. What the fuck is going on?

"No, get out of here," Anna screams through the comms. I'm not fucking leaving them behind. "Get back to the cabin."

Fuck that. I'm going after them.

The earth vibrates as an explosion sends me backward. My legs buckle beneath me, sending my body crashing to the ground. "Anna!" I scream. "Claire," my voice is hoarse as I manage to lift to my knees and try to push myself up.

"Ben, what's happening? I'm blind. I'm sending in the drones."

"I don't know, I can't see anything."

I hear a helicopter approaching and land nearby. With everything that I have, I push up off the ground and run back to the truck. I take the rifle and set it up on the hood of the truck. I look through the scope to see that piece of shit Vang victoriously emerge from the helicopter. My aim is nowhere as good as Anna's and there's no way I'll be able to take him out from here.

"I should be surprised, but I'm not," I hear his voice come through the comms.

"I'll take the shot," I say to Agent as I try to calm myself.

"You only have one shot, and if you aren't successful then you're both as good as dead."

"Fuck," I grumble as I weigh up my options. If I take the shot and miss, I'll never get my girl back. But if I don't take it, there's no way I'll know where he takes her.

Vang beckons one of his men before squatting and stroking his hand over my girl's cheek. "Why are you here, Anna?" I want to tear his fucking arms off his body. How dare he touch my girl the way he's doing. "Get her to the helicopter," Vang instructs his men.

"What's this?" Vang's security says as he plucks the comms from her ear. He shows Vang who automatically looks around the premises. Vang's man scoops Anna's lifeless body up and swings her over his shoulder.

"Fuck," I hear Anna groan. Relief washes over me with her sweet though painful cry. She's not dead, she's alive. He drops the earpiece and crushes it under his foot.

"Ben," Agent says in my ear.

"Yeah."

"I'm sorry, but..." he pauses for a moment.

"They killed her, didn't they?"

"Yeah." I run my hand through my hair and attempt to refocus. "They had the security looped, and I didn't see it until the last minute. When it broke the loop, I saw your sister was already..." My gut tightens with what I'm expecting his next words to be. "I'm sorry."

I take a moment to clear my head. I get into the driver's seat of the truck and head back to Anna's cabin. "Can you um..." I start but stop when I don't know what to say to Agent.

"What do you need?"

I drive carefully but fast to get back to Anna's cabin so I can form some kind of game plan. I need to figure out where he's taking my girl and get her back. "Vang has several properties," I start. "Can you hack into all their security systems and see where he's holding her?"

"I'm already on it. I've hacked into the GPS on his phone and the helicopter is heading toward the castle."

"Where the raid was?"

"Yeah," Agent replies. "I'm also in their security feeds and the castle is swarming with at least eighty men."

"Fuck," I grumble. "I'm heading back to the cabin now."

"I know." I shouldn't be surprised that Agent can see my every move. "You're going to need an override to get into her cabin. I'll wait until you arrive and scan your prints."

My prints? Shit, that could be a problem. They don't know who I am, but Agent will figure it out soon enough. I should tell Agent now, but I'd rather Anna hear it from me before Agent does. "There's something you need to know," I say to Agent as I speed toward the cabin.

"What?"

"Have you heard of the Pace family?"

"Really?" Agent asks in a patronizing tone.

"Claire and I head it." There's silence on the other end of the connection. "Agent?"

The pause is bitter and making my heart beat faster. "If they took 15 because of you, I'll fucking kill you myself." Agent's anger is not unjustified. But his tone is eerily even and deadly.

"I'll get her back, but I'll need your help."

"You fucking better get 15 back," he warns.

I drive down the makeshift dirt road toward her cabin and park right outside. "I'm at the cabin."

"I fucking know," Agent snaps. "I told you; I can see you. Place your finger on the pad." I jump out of the truck and head up to the front door where I place my thumb on the pad. It takes about sixty seconds, but the door finally clicks open. "You're in, I'm going to get the live feed up on her laptop so you can see what I see when I get her in view." Agent hangs up abruptly.

I deserve his wrath. Anna is a one-of-a-kind woman, and I know Agent is reliant on her for so much. She's his family, like he's hers. I take a moment to settle my erratic thoughts and pick up the phone to call Emily. "What's happening, Ben?" she answers the call.

"Emily, I need you to sit down."

"What is it?"

"Vang killed Claire," I say bluntly but with a breaking voice. "I'm sorry. I couldn't keep her safe," I say in a smaller voice.

Emily doesn't reply, not with words. The silence from her side is filled with tears that rapidly turn into sobs. I sit on the armchair and hang my head as I rub at the tightness across my forehead. "Ben," she finally whispers.

"Yeah."

"Kill him."

"He took Anna."

Her sobs stop and she inhales deeply. "Find him, and fucking kill him. Torture the fuck out of him, slice his tongue out of his mouth, stick an explosive up his ass, I don't care, Ben. I want him dead."

"I will," I say. "I promise you, Emily, I'll fucking kill him."

"What do you need me to do?"

"For now, stay where you are. Remember, live on cash and if you think someone is closing in, get rid of the phone and get out from where you are."

"Okay," she says.

The laptop sparks alive and there's an image of the castle. "I have to go."

"I need you to keep in touch with me."

"I will." Emily hangs up, and the instant she does, Agent is in my ear.

"She seems agitated," he says flatly. He's angry at me for hiding the truth about my family. "Anna's definitely at the castle. Look on the laptop."

The screen is split into four sections. There's visual but no audio. In the top right square is Anna on a bed where she's shackled and appears lifeless. The other three squares show various areas of the castle swamped with guards. They all appear to be hyperaware, as if they're waiting for an army to turn up. "Fuck," I grumble.

"There are too many of them," Agent says. "Too many for just you to go in and get her."

"There's no way?" I ask. "I'll take the smallest possibility."

"No, you won't. This is 15's life we're talking about. You betrayed her once. I'm not going to green-light a suicide mission that'll kill her in the process."

"I'm trying to do the right thing," I argue with the faceless Agent.

"Then try harder."

I know I've done wrong by Agent and he's protective of her. "Is there any way I can get in and get her out?"

"I'm looking at the blueprints now," he sounds somewhat calmer. "Vang has guards everywhere, and judging by their weapons, they're waiting for someone."

"Probably me."

"Definitely you. Maybe I can trade you for 15," he adds with a sting to his voice. So much for the calm.

"I care about her, Agent," I finally say.

"That's why you lied to her."

"I didn't lie, I just didn't tell her."

"An omission of the truth is still a betrayal and a lie." Fuck. "Look," he says after a tense few seconds. "You being a dick isn't going to get 15 back." I lift my brows and shake my head. Agent's anger toward me is justified. I should've told her the truth when she opened up about who she was. I thought I could keep my secret, but now it's come back to bite me on the ass. "I'm going to keep an eye on the castle and see if there's an opportunity for us to get her out. Keep this phone on you. I'll be in contact." Agent ends the call, leaving me feeling fucking helpless.

I got her into this mess, I have to get her out. I'll trade them, my life for hers. But Vang isn't a man of his word. He'd kill us both and he'll have ended 15—the most lethal woman in the world. He'll kill me and my family business.

This is fucked.

Day two of Anna being held by Vang, and Agent has managed to get audio and video of where Anna is. I watch the screen and see Anna stirs from time to time, but she hasn't woken. My jaw clenches as I fixate on the screen and watch the guard in her room touch my girl. He runs his hand up and down her leg, then walks over to the door and opens it. He stands in the hallway for a few seconds before he reenters the room and heads over to the bed.

The fucker licks his lips as he trails his hand up her leg. He opens his pants and shoves his hand inside.

"Fuck," I grumble as he masturbates while his free hand touches my woman. The phone rings and I lift it to my ear. "Yeah," I say with a tight voice.

"Are you watching?" Agent asks.

A violent explosion is simmering deep inside me. There's a pounding in my ears that matches the thumping in my chest. "I'm watching," I say through a clenched jaw.

"When this is over and we have her back, you kill him."

"I promise you, I'm going to kill them all."

"Good." Agent disconnects, leaving me to watch this sick fuck pleasure himself while he's groping my woman. I find myself biting the inside of my cheek as fury charges through me.

This fucker will certainly die.

"It's been three days, Agent. I can't sit around waiting for something to happen." I watch the screen as Vang enters the room Anna's being held in.

"She's worth more than that." Vang's on the phone with someone. "She'll work for you and end up being one of your best earners. I can promise you that."

"Track the call," I say to Agent.

"I'm on it."

"Nope. I'm not taking that for her. How many times have we done business?" Vang says with anger. "She's worth more than the others." He walks back and forth in front of the filthy bed she's on. He stops and looks down at her, brushing some hair from her face. "No, she won't be as good an earner as someone who's ten or eleven, but she'll bring in good money for you. Besides, you owe me." He begins pacing and again, then stops and smiles. "Good." He ends the call and shoves the phone back in his pocket.

"Tell me you got the trace?"

"I didn't."

"Fuck," I groan as I stand and walk away from the computer. What's Vang done?

It's been four days and I'm barely holding on. I've only had moments of sleep because I've been consumed by the computer screen and watching over Anna. She's been stirring, like she's trying to wake up. It's only a matter of time before she wakes from her state. I feel sorry for the fuckers who've been holding her.

I head over to the kitchen to make myself a coffee when I hear Anna's voice. "Shit," I say and rush over to the laptop. I sit and watch as she stirs. I lift the phone and call Agent. "She's waking," I say.

"I'm already on it. I'm listening and recording."

"Where am I?" she asks as she wets her lips. Her voice is gruff and jagged and filled with uncertainty.

The guard who's in there with her stands and takes his phone out of his pocket. He dials and holds it up to his ear. "She's waking." He plonks his ass back on the chair.

"Where am I?" Anna repeats as she attempts to look around the room. The man slowly stands and makes his way to the foot of the bed. He draws his weapon and points it at Anna. My teeth grind together as I watch him aim at a restrained woman. He's just made his way on my shit list, too. It takes Anna another moment or so before she gains her composure.

"This guy has a death sentence," Agent says.

"I'm strapped down," my girl says to the guard pointing his gun at her. Anna's looking around the room as the door opens. Her head turns to see who's entering the room.

Vang walks past the guard and places his hand on the barrel, lowering it. "Anna Moore, it's good to see you again."

He has no idea who she is.

Thank God.

Anna's features are tight as she watches Vang carefully. "How long have I been out?"

Vang grabs the chair and tugs it to be beside the bed. "Four days." He sits on the chair and folds his hands in his lap carefully. Asshole thinks he's in control, but he has no idea who he's up against. "What were you doing at the building, Anna?"

"She's not going to give him anything," Agent says.

I lean closer to the laptop as I watch the exchange between Vang and Anna. She turns her head and closes her mouth. The hammering of my heart is making my breath quick and sharp. She's the controlled assassin, and I'm the arms dealer. Her control's far superior to what mine could ever be.

"What were you doing there?" Vang's voice lowers to a menacing, cold tone. She continues to ignore him. Vang unlaces his fingers and lifts his right hand to place over her throat. Even from the grainy video I can see he's tightening his grip and cutting off her air supply.

"Jesus," I say as I stand and take a step backward. "I need to get there."

"And do what? Get you both killed?" Agent replies.

"Why were you there?" He tightens his grip, but Anna doesn't react to his cruelty. He finally releases his hand, making Anna gasp for air. "I asked you a question."

It takes Anna a few seconds to take in a few deep breaths. She finally turns to stare at him and grins. "Sleepwalking," she says with an obvious hint of sass.

Vang balls his hand into a fist and punches her in the jaw.

I inhale a sharp breath and find my arms straining as I close my hands into fists. "She's going to kill him," Agent says.

"If I don't do it first." I hate seeing her being hurt and being completely useless.

"Big man, beating up a woman while she's tied up. Good for you, you hero," she torments Vang.

"Stop," I whisper.

"Leave her, she knows what she's doing."

"I can't exactly stop her, can I, Agent?"

"You're going to end up like your friend, Claire Pace. I knew if I captured one of the heads of the Pace family, then at least her brother would come after her. *Fucking family*. But no. You came instead."

"Shit," Agent murmurs.

I feel like I haven't been able to take a breath for the last few days. But now, I'm relieved she knows, although this isn't how I wanted her to find out. I wanted to be the one to tell her. "Who's Claire Pace?" Anna asks with a cold, stoic tone.

I know Anna, she's playing Vang. She's probably laying there calculating her next move all while extracting as much information as she can. She's shrewd and cold, maybe even a sociopath.

"The Pace family caused me to lose millions in revenue when they fucked up that shipment. Not to mention they're causing me more problems with their import and export of artillery. A fucking family of influence. I killed one half of them, and now, I need to find the brother and kill him."

"He's waiting for you, that's why he's armed himself with so many of his men. They're on guard for you, not her," Agent says.

I know. "I have to make this right."

"You're not going to do anything stupid, Ben. You can't go and give yourself up for her. You know he'll kill both of you."

Agent is right. I need to face Anna and cop whatever wrath she's going to rightfully inflict on me. I can't let Vang get that opportunity first.

"Fucking liar," she snaps at him. "You'll say whatever you want to get your way."

Vang releases a demonic gurgle resembling a heartless laugh. "You had no idea you were fucking the enemy, did you?"

Anna licks her lips and shakes her head. She pointedly stares at his crotch. "It's better than fucking a guy with a pencil dick."

"Ben Pace is the enemy here, not me." Anna doesn't reply to Vang. He stands and holds his hand out to the guard in the room. It's in that second, I notice he's drawing up liquid from a heated spoon.

"Shit," Agent whispers.

Vang sits on the side of the bed and flicks the syringe before handing it to the guard and swaps it for a torniquet. "He knows exactly what he's doing."

"Vang knows she's powerless and he's making a point to her that he's in control."

"I'm going to fucking kill him."

"You'll like this," Vang says as he ties the torniquet around her upper arm, then proceeds to slap the inside of her forearm. "You've made me some money, so thank you."

Anna snarls as she stares into Vang's eyes. Her jaw clenches and her nose crinkles. "I don't think I've ever seen her this angry," Agent says.

"I'll find you, Katsuo, and I'm going to hurt you," she says with absolute certainty.

Vang laughs and inserts the needle into her arm. "You're going to a place that there's no coming back from."

"Keep looking over your shoulder," Anna warns.

Vang doesn't take her seriously, because he has no idea who Anna is. "Good luck with that." He stands from the bed and issues instructions to move Anna onto her side so she doesn't choke on her own vomit.

Anna turns her head to Vang and says, "I found you once, I'll find you again." Her tone is unnervingly controlled. The drug takes over her body and she instantly softens, becoming a malleable shadow of her naturally assertive self.

I stare at the computer for another moment or so before standing and walking away. I link my hands and place them on my head as I pace back and forth trying to figure out how I'm going to get her back, and end Vang—once and for all. He can't continue breathing. I'll call in every favor I possibly can to find the fucker. My chest tightens as I focus on the pain I'll be bringing to Vang. I don't care what happens to me, I need him dead.

"Ben..." Agent calls me back to the now.

"What?"

"We've got a bigger problem."

"What?"

"15's being shipped."

I run back to the computer and look at the screen. "Where's she going?" I walk over to her weapons room. "Open the door." I'm going to arm myself with everything possible and go in there with all guns blazing. As long as I get Anna out, I don't give a damn if I die. "Open the fucking door," I yell at Agent because I know he's able to access the code to get me in.

"Ben, you can't take the weapons where she's going."

I pause and look up at one of the security cameras. I walk toward it and stare up. "Where are they taking her?"

"I'm getting you and your sister on a flight. I'll make all the arrangements."

"Where are they taking her?" I repeat for the last time.

"Ben, she's already in transit. She's going to..."

I hold my breath as Agent informs me.

Fuck, this is going to make it much harder to get her back. Not impossible though.

First thing first is to get my girl back. Then I'll take care of Vang.

CHAPTER EIGHTEEN

ANNA

My head is fuzzy, and every time I start to come out of the drug-induced haze they have me in, they inject me with more. Not enough to overdose me, but enough to keep me compliant and force an addiction.

I'm not sure who *they* are yet, but when I figure it out, they're going to be the first I take down. Then I'll track down Katsuo and make him hurt for what he's done.

My list is forever growing, but that's okay because I have the gift of patience. I'll get myself out of this situation, and when I do, I'll destroy every fucker who's had a part in this.

Every single one of them.

Suddenly, my body shakes as the pull of the drugs begins to take over. Although my body is hurting, my mind is clearing. I should be begging for more drugs, but my head is deflated by Ben's betrayal.

He lied to me.

No, it wasn't a lie because I never asked him. But he neglected to tell me something that potentially could've changed the rescue mission for Claire. I can't bring myself to hate him for not telling me, but I can't let it go either.

Shit, the moment of lucidity is quickly clouding with an overwhelming desire for another hit. My stomach contracts, and I close my eyes to regulate my erratic breaths.

The motion of the van I'm in isn't helping with the tightness in my chest or my stomach that's curdling. "I need some more," I yell. Fuck, no. I need to be strong. I have to break the bonds this toxic drug has over me.

But I'm losing the battle.

I lift my bound feet and try to smash the side of the van. "More!" I scream at the fuckers who've taken me.

There are two men in the front and can hear them whispering something, but I can't exactly make out what they're saying. The van finally stops, and then I hear footsteps approaching down its side. They're loud as they walk on a gravelly surface. The back door slides open, and I turn to see who the person is. It's dark outside, making it hard for me to focus on the person, but I'm met with a closed fist to the face, making my head thump with pain.

"This'll shut you up, bitch." I feel the sharp sting of a needle in my hip.

He's not injecting me with heroin, it's something else.

Instantly, I close my eyes and fall into a deep sleep.

The air is hot and humid, causing me to wake in a sweaty mess. I try to move but my wrists are zip tied together while my ankles burn from the rope. My mouth is dry and I try to wet my lips as I blink several times.

Where am I?

I turn and notice the inside of the van is different. It's cleaner and more sterile. Have I been moved?

My head is fuzzy yet thumping with a god-awful throb, starting at the base of my neck all the way up to my temples. "Where am I?" my voice is strained and tight. It's barely louder than a whisper. I try and swallow several times, but my mouth isn't producing enough saliva.

My entire body is protesting as I attempt to dislodge the shackles keeping me captive.

The van jerks to a complete halt, and I twist to see where I've been taken. The windowless back makes it hard to tell what time of the day it is, and the fact I've been in a drug haze makes it even harder to know what day it is.

The side door rolls open, and I'm blasted with the sun's brightness. I squint so I'm not directly looking out into the vivid illumination. A man I haven't seen before stands at the doorway sleazily gawking at me from top to bottom, then back up again. He has a toothpick in his mouth that he rolls from side to side. "She's gonna be one mighty earner," he says in that same foreign accent. I can't quite pick it though, it's not an English accent but it's similar. "Get her out," he instructs someone.

He steps back and two other men come into focus. One tapes my mouth, while the other maneuvers me closer to the door. There's no use in fighting or screaming because like this, I'm fairly useless.

I'm going to have to wait until my limbs aren't restricted and I have a fair idea of where I am.

"She's a pretty one," the guy who put tape over my mouth says. "A little chunky in the thighs, but we know the clientele are gonna like her considering she's got a bit of meat on her bones." He sits me up and pushes me forward.

My eyes have adjusted to the light, and I look around trying to gain my bearings.

The van is parked in a tight alleyway. The street is lined with old, almost cobblestone, pavers. "I've seen prettier," the other one says as he hoists me up over his shoulder.

What the fuck did I just see?

He walks with me slung over his shoulder, like I'm nothing, in through a back gate. I lift my head to look around me.

Wait... is that what I think it is? The Harbour Bridge?

Holy shit. I've been smuggled into Australia.

Specifically, Sydney.

My entire body is engulfed in a blaze of anger. My heart rate races, my pulse quickens, and my teeth grind causing a sharp pain to radiate through my jaw.

You fuckers better be ready for what I'm about to bring.

Far from the end.

But, who is...

Epilogue

Adele

S tanding in the front of the foggy mirror, I swipe my hand across it. My dark, wet hair falls limply down to my shoulders. The exhaust fan in the bathroom is making an irritating, off-pitch clicking as it turns slowly.

I look up at it, distracted by the stupid noise and make a mental note to have it replaced. I take several deep breaths to overcome my annoyance before returning my gaze to the mirror.

The steel-framed edge of the mirror holds the dated photo of a woman. She looks similar to me. We have the same hair, the same eyes, and even our face shape is similar. My body is curvier than hers, though anyone can see the resemblance. It's crystal clear we're related somehow.

I never knew who she was, but I found this photo when I was on an assignment. I was investigating an assassination. I couldn't believe who this woman was to me. It took me weeks to finally come to terms with it.

I feel like I'm chasing an enigma, a ghost who's constantly just out of my reach.

I'll find everything out. I have to. I refuse to rest until I know the truth.

But, for now, I have to get ready for work.

Being on my motorcycle is when my brain is most active. Thoughts flood my head, and I can't help thinking about everything.

When Ben disappeared, I called my superiors—as per regulations—to let them know. To say they weren't impressed is certainly an understatement. I haven't been able to track Ben's phone, because it's been turned off. I haven't even been able to find his car. I don't know where he is. He and Anna both have vanished, as if they never existed to start with. But now, Katsuo Vang is gone, Anna is gone, and so is Ben. This is nothing short of a shitshow.

My superiors are demanding to see me in person so we can make a game plan for what to do. That's code for I'm about to walk into a world of pain.

My stomach contracts as I approach the building, and I dread what's about to happen. There's a sour taste in my mouth as I pull up to the driveway. I can feel sweat beading on the back of my neck where my helmet meets my hairline. I won't show them weakness though, because they'll eat me alive if I do.

I pull up to the garage and press the button attached to the black swipe pad. "Remove your helmet," the male voice announces in a humdrum, bored drone. I take off my helmet and look up at the camera. It takes about thirty seconds, but the garage door slowly lifts.

I make my way down the steep driveway and park my bike near the elevator doors. I use the kickstand to keep my bike upright and sling my helmet over the handlebars.

I turn and look at the elevator before taking a deep breath to prepare myself for whatever is about to happen. Will I be met by wrath? Yelling? A crippling fear makes my hands tremble.

Pull yourself together, Adele.

I press the up button and wait until the doors open before stepping in. I press the number I need and step back, trying to make myself as small as possible. My heart is hammering in my chest, and my breathing is fast and erratic. I squeeze my eyes shut as I take deep breaths in an attempt to calm the choking tightness in my gut.

The doors ping open and I look out into the corridor. I head to the last room with its double doors and stand for a moment. I lift my chin and pull my shoulders back. I knock twice and only have to wait for a few seconds before I hear "Enter."

I tuck the stray hairs around my face back behind my ears and open the doors. I glance at the handful of people sitting at the conference table. They stop talking and focus on me. I recognize each person in the room. There are bottles of water, empty and bunched together, along with numerous coffee mugs and stacks of papers filling the table.

The dark circles beneath most their eyes tell me they've been here for a while. The papers, discarded food containers, and their overall disheveled appearance confirms my thoughts.

"Special Agent Adele Petrov, we're glad you could join us." Like I had much of a choice. FBI Assistant Director Lomax gestures toward an unoccupied chair.

"Thank you," I reply as I walk over, pull out the seat, and sit. I acknowledge everyone around the room.

"Special Agent Tyler Lewis has filled us in about what he knows from his time with Katsuo Vang, now we need an update on what you know about Ben Pearson and Anna Moore."

I take a deep breath and compose myself as I sit straighter in the seat. I push everything else out of my mind. My focus right now is Ben Pearson and Anna Moore. I push the photo of the woman I've been carrying with me for the last few months out of my mind. *For now.*

I let her name make one last appearance until Ben Pearson is dealt with.

Be patient because I'll find your killer. And when I do, I'll make them pay. I wish I knew you before you were taken from me.

I love you forever, my dearest mother, *Natalia.*

MARGARET MCHEYZER

Email: hit_149@yahoo.com

info@margaretmcheyzer.com

Facebook: Margaret McHeyzer Author

TikTok: Margaretmcheyzerauthor

Printed in Great Britain
by Amazon

26676530R00119